“Cut it out...”

Ben whispered close to Mandy’s ear, “You’re going to make me start laughing, too.”

“Sorry,” she whispered as she looked up.

Her laughter froze when their eyes met. The brightness staring back at him stole what was left of his breath. And from the way she was gazing up at him, he knew he wasn’t alone.

Come on lungs, breathe!

Honestly, how could someone forget how to breathe? But as Mandy looked up at Ben’s face, it was as if someone had flipped the switch on her respiratory system to Off.

Damn, he was even more handsome up close. Thank goodness they were in near darkness. If he looked this good hiding in the shadows, this type of proximity in full light might just be her end.

His mouth parted, and she felt her traitorous body start to move toward him...

Dear Reader,

One of the hallmarks of a good romance story is that the hero and heroine have to overcome some significant obstacle to achieve their happily-ever-after. Sometimes that obstacle is so big that it doesn't seem possible for them to get past it.

Such is the case for Mandy and Ben in *The Rancher's Surprise Baby*. And yet true love always finds a way to change the hearts and minds that need to be changed.

I hope you enjoy Mandy and Ben's journey to their happily-ever-after.

All the best,

Trish

THE RANCHER'S SURPRISE BABY

TRISH MILBURN

Recycling programs for this product may not exist in your area.

ISBN-13: 978-0-373-75762-6

The Rancher's Surprise Baby

This edition published by arrangement with Harlequin Books S.A.

For questions and comments about the quality of this book, please contact us at CustomerService@Harlequin.com.

Printed in U.S.A.

Trish Milburn writes contemporary romance for the Harlequin Western Romance line. She's a two-time Golden Heart® Award winner, a fan of walks in the woods and road trips, and a big geek girl, including being a dedicated Whovian and Browncoat. And from her earliest memories, she's been a fan of Westerns, be they historical or contemporary. There's nothing quite like a cowboy hero.

Books by Trish Milburn

Harlequin Western Romance

Blue Falls, Texas

Her Perfect Cowboy
Having the Cowboy's Baby
Marrying the Cowboy
The Doctor's Cowboy
Her Cowboy Groom
The Heart of a Cowboy
Home on the Ranch
A Rancher to Love
The Cowboy Takes a Wife
In the Rancher's Arms

Harlequin American Romance

The Teagues of Texas

The Cowboy's Secret Son
Cowboy to the Rescue
The Cowboy Sheriff

Visit the Author Profile page
at Harlequin.com for more titles.

Chapter One

Forget out of the frying pan and into the fire. Stepping out of the arctic air-conditioning of the Primrose Café into the suffocating heat of a Texas afternoon in August was like drilling a hole in the North Pole deep enough to fall straight into hell.

Mandy Richardson hurried toward the edge of the parking lot, where she'd nabbed the last spot in front of Blue Falls' oldest eating establishment and the hub of town gossip. In the time it took for her to pick up dinner for her mom and herself, she'd heard that Franny Stokes had gone on a blind date with a guy she met online through some dating site for senior citizens, Bernie Shumaker had launched his newest in a string of business attempts—wind chimes made from everything from silverware to driftwood this time—and Loren Whitman's grandson had caught a fish so big that he fell out of their boat into the middle of the lake. To add insult to embarrassment, the fish got away.

Honestly, a dunk in the middle of Blue Falls Lake would feel really good right about now. In addition to it being hot as blazes outside, her feet ached from being on them since early that morning. It'd been another busy day at A Good Yarn, the yarn and sewing shop her best friend, Devon, owned and where Mandy worked. The combination of the tail end of summer vacationing combined with it being the weekend of the local monthly rodeo had filled the downtown shops from the time they'd opened their doors at 8:00 a.m. Good for business but tiring. All she wanted was to eat her fried chicken, drink about a gallon of her mom's homemade lemonade and prop up her poor feet. A foot massage would be fantastic, preferably one given by an incredibly hunky guy, but she figured that, sadly, wasn't in her immediate future.

The sound of squealing tires, followed immediately by a bang and the screeching sound of metal on metal, caused her to startle so much she fumbled the food containers she held.

"No, no, no," she said as she tried to maintain her hold, but all she managed to do was flick the bottom container open as it fell. The top one followed its twin to the newly paved parking lot. She'd swear she heard the chicken sizzle as it sat there amid a sea of splattered mashed potatoes and green beans.

As she lamented the loss of her dinner, she glanced up to figure out what had precipitated it. That was when she noticed half of that metal-on-metal sound had come from her car. The other half belonged to the pickup truck all up in her car's grille.

"You have got to be kidding me," she said as she shook her head slowly in disbelief. "I know I'm a good person. Karma, you took a wrong turn."

She looked down at the mess of food at her feet. She needed to clean it up, but first things first. As she approached her car, the driver's side door of the pickup opened and the first thing she saw was a cowboy boot and the bottom of a pair of jeans. When the man stepped out from behind the door, looking dazed, she immediately recognized him. She'd bet her meager savings that there wasn't a woman alive in Blue Falls—young, old, single, married or even half-blind—who hadn't at some point in time given tall, blond, blue-eyed Ben Hartley a second look. And a third. And…

Oh, stop thinking about how dang handsome he is and ask him why he decided to have his truck give your car an unwanted smacker.

As she drew closer, he shook his head as if trying to clear it. Was he drunk? DUI seemed to be more TJ Malpin's thing, not one of the raised-right Hartley clan.

He glanced at where his truck had hit the car then up at her. His forehead wrinkled for a moment, as if he was trying to figure out who she was, before it seemed to click. Maybe he *was* drunk. Or high. Though neither of those options rang true at all.

"Are you okay?" she asked, suddenly wondering if maybe he'd banged his head and given himself a concussion. He did have a red mark on the edge of his forehead.

He pointed at her little compact. "Is this your car?"

"Yeah. But you didn't answer my question."

"I'm fine."

He didn't seem fine. He seemed downright addled. As if trying to piece together what had happened, he looked at his truck for a moment before turning back toward her.

"I know this will sound as if I'm off my rocker, but a bird made me do it."

For a long moment she just stared at him, wondering if the heat had cooked her brain so much that she was hearing things incorrectly. "A bird made you do it?"

Several seconds passed before he seemed to realize the absurdity of what he was saying, but then he straightened and appeared more confident in the truth of it.

"I had the windows down, and all of a sudden something hit me in the side of the head. I jerked the steering wheel without even thinking." He rubbed at the reddened spot above his temple. "I think I swatted it. Right before the crash there were feathers in my face."

If her car wasn't sitting there crunched, she'd have a difficult time deciding whether to laugh or call to have someone take him for a mental evaluation. But then a racket behind him drew her attention, and suddenly a pigeon flew out of the open window of his truck.

"See, not crazy," he said.

She had to admit the pigeon looked almost as addled as Ben.

"That leaves me with one pressing question," she said.

"How bad your car is damaged?"

She glanced at her poor little car. "Well, yes, but more important, why in the name of all that's holy you were driving with the windows down on a day like today."

"The air-conditioning went out halfway to town."

She couldn't help the laugh that burst out of her. "Not your day, is it?"

For a moment, he looked at her as if she'd taken leave of her senses, as if she'd been the one addled by a pigeon. But then he offered a hint of a smile. "Nope."

"Me neither."

"A PIGEON? THAT'S THE story you're going with?" Greg Bozeman asked Ben as he hitched up Mandy Richardson's car to his tow truck. The little thing hadn't stood a chance against Ben's pickup. The truck had a nice dent in the grille, but at least it was still operational. Mandy's car, not so much.

"I can vouch for the pigeon story," Mandy said. "Saw it fly out of the truck looking as if it'd had a few too many drinks at the Frothy Stein."

Greg laughed. "You're not living this one down."

"If I didn't have such a headache right now, I'd think of some snappy comeback," Ben said.

He caught a sudden look of concern on Mandy's face.

"Do you think you should have your head checked out?" she asked.

Greg howled even more at that, and Ben gave him a dirty look.

"No, the only thing that would make this worse is strolling into the ER and telling them I got beaned by a pigeon."

"You could have a concussion."

"I've had a concussion before. This ain't one."

Greg walked toward the driver's side of the tow

truck. "Bring your truck by the shop and I'll check out your AC for free just for making my day with this pigeon story."

Greg was saved from being the recipient of a rude gesture because Ben was enough of a gentleman not to be that crude in front of Mandy. He knew her, but not that well. He'd already crunched her car. He didn't need to risk offending her sensibilities on top of it.

As Greg drove off with Mandy's car in tow, Ben wondered exactly how long it would be before everyone in the county—hell, the entirety of the Hill Country—knew about his bird encounter. If someone had snapped a photo, he'd no doubt be the top story in the next edition of the *Blue Falls Gazette*.

He turned back to where Mandy stood holding up her ponytail and fanning her neck with her other hand. Her face was flushed with the heat, even though the sun was sinking in the western sky. Not that it cooled off that much after sunset this time of year.

"Where were you headed before a crazy birdman ran into your car?" He'd noticed her cleaning up a couple of spilled to-go containers while he'd waited for Greg to arrive with the tow truck.

"My mom's place, but all I want to do now is go home and collapse. It's been one of those days. I told Mom we'd get together a different day."

"Let me give you a ride."

"Okay, if you're sure your truck is safe to drive."

He placed his palm atop the hood of the truck. "She has a new dent, but she's drivable. Sorry, but you got the raw end of the deal today."

"At least I didn't suffer a bird to the head."

He smiled. "True. I don't recommend it."

They climbed into the truck, and that little skirt with the big bright flowers she was wearing rode up her thighs a bit. She didn't seem to notice or care, but that few extra inches of skin caused it to grow even hotter inside the already roasting cab.

"Sorry I can't offer AC, but at least we'll have some moving air in a minute."

"I might just have you drop me at the lake so I can jump in."

The last thing he needed was the image of her with that skirt and her light blue sleeveless top plastered to her body.

Damn, maybe he did have a concussion. He'd never thought about Mandy that way before. Heck, he hadn't thought about her much at all. She was just someone he knew casually. Or maybe it was seeing his older brother, Neil, having a hard time keeping his hands off Arden, his fiancée, that had him thinking it'd been a while since he'd gone out on a date. But wrecking a woman's car seemed like a bad precursor to asking her out to dinner.

Asking Mandy out? That was it, he was going home and sticking his head in his mom's freezer, maybe pressing a bag of green peas against his aching temple.

"So, where to?" he asked, focusing on the road in front of him.

"Actually, out toward your place. The former Webster ranch."

He looked over at her. "You bought the Cedar Creek? Maybe I need to start working in a yarn shop."

"Yes, I'm sure you know loads about yarn and knitting needles." She shook her head. "I only bought a couple of acres on the creek. They subdivided so they could sell off the land quicker."

"Huh. I'm surprised one of those bigwigs looking to invest in large tracts for hobby ranches didn't snap it up. We had one sniffing around ours until my soon-to-be sister-in-law sent him packing with the threat of some not-so-nice press coverage."

"Well, I heard that was a secondary reason for subdividing. The Websters wanted their place to go to people who could afford a more reasonable price tag and appreciate it more. Got the feeling they didn't like rich 'bigwigs' too much."

He laughed at that. "I always did like the Websters. Hated they had to sell, but they had a rough time this past year."

Ranching was always a touch-and-go way to make a living. That was why he and his brothers and sisters did their best to keep expenses low and to bring in other income to make sure the Rocking Heart stayed afloat for their parents—and for future generations of Hartleys. Of course, he wasn't going to be providing any of those munchkins—even though his family didn't know that. Luckily, his sister Angel already had a daughter, and he'd bet Neil and Arden popped out a few rug rats before long.

"Do you need to stop anywhere before we leave town?" he asked Mandy. "Grab some dinner?"

"Nah. I might just pour a glass of wine and sit in the creek."

"Make it a beer and that doesn't sound half-bad."

"You're welcome to the creek, but I don't have any beer."

"I better stay away from the creek. The way my day's going, I'd probably fall and drown in an inch of water."

"I'd save you. I might have to leave you there if you're unconscious, but I'd at least roll you faceup."

He laughed. "How very kind of you. Have to say you're being pretty nice to the guy who crashed into your car."

She shrugged. "Being mad wouldn't make it any less crunched. Plus, at least I didn't get whacked in the head by a bird."

Her smile transformed her face from merely pretty to stunning. Why had he never noticed how gorgeous she was before? Perspiration made damp wisps of her hair curl around the edges of her face, and he thought maybe there was a dusting of freckles across the bridge of her nose. He experienced the oddest urge to lean closer to find out. Of course that was a bad idea on a lot of levels, not the least of which was he'd probably end up driving his truck into some other stationary object. Or she'd whack him on the other side of his head.

He jerked his attention back to the road. That damned pigeon had obviously knocked his brain loose, causing it to bounce around inside his skull.

Mandy leaned her head over on her forearm where it rested along the open window, letting the wind whip the loose strands of her hair. She closed her eyes in a way that made him realize how tired she must be after a day of work then standing out in the heat while they dealt with first Deputy Conner Murphy, who'd also had a not-well-hidden chuckle at the bird attack story, then Greg. For a moment, he thought maybe she'd fallen asleep. But then she opened her eyes and pointed ahead.

"Turn at the next road on the left."

He turned onto a smaller county road and then into a new gravel drive flanked by lines of cedar trees. Through them he spotted the trickle of the creek, one that ran wider, deeper and faster during spring rains like the creek on his family's ranch. Up ahead, a little wooden shed sat with a miniature front porch pointed toward the creek. When he noticed that the gravel drive ended next to it, he glanced over at Mandy in confusion.

"Where's your house?"

She pointed toward the shed. "That's it."

"Ha-ha, very funny. The pigeon didn't hit me that hard."

"No, seriously, that's it."

"You live in a shed?"

She turned partially toward him. "It's not a shed. It's a tiny house."

It was tiny, all right. How did she fit anything in there? He didn't think it was any bigger than his bedroom.

"Come on, I'll give you the ten-cent tour," she said as he stopped in a wider gravel area that appeared to be where she normally parked and turned her car around.

"More like the ten-second tour," he said as he put the truck in Park and cut the engine.

Mandy smiled. "That, too."

His boots made a crunching sound on the gravel when he stepped out of the truck. The low slant of the sun made her little spot on the creek look appealing, even if she did live in a house that would probably give him claustrophobia despite the fact he'd never suffered from it before. He noticed the little porch held a bright blue metal chair, a pot of purple and white flowers and a small metal wind chime. Next to the front step sat one of those concrete yard ornaments, this one a green frog wearing a crown.

He pointed at the frog. "Do I even want to ask?"

"I kiss him every day in case he's a prince in disguise."

He looked over at her. "Are you sure you aren't the one who got a bird to the noggin?"

"I'm not a believer in taking life too seriously," she said.

Obviously. But he had to admit there was something really appealing about her attitude.

As she headed toward the front of the little house and he got a good look at her bare legs, he thought they were pretty darn appealing, too. Whether or not she really did kiss that stupid frog every day, she did now, then stood back and watched it as if it might really turn into a prince. If it did, he was changing his mind and driving himself straight to the emergency room.

"Darn, still no luck." She smiled at Ben and practically skipped up the step to the porch.

"You ain't right, Mandy Richardson."

"I take that as a compliment."

If she only knew a couple of the other compliments that had popped into his mind, she might hit the other side of his head with a frying pan.

By the time she unlocked the front door, he'd stepped up onto the porch behind her. When she opened the door, a blast of cold air hit him. She stepped inside and took the three steps necessary to bring her to the small AC unit in one of the windows. She bent and kissed the thing.

"You go around kissing inanimate objects often?"

She glanced at him. "Only when they produce cold air or might turn into a prince."

He shook his head. "Not right at all."

When she laughed, it seemed as if it was as much at herself as his words.

"Would you like something to drink?" she asked as she moved toward a small fridge. "I'm afraid your choices are wine, water or cranberry juice."

"I'll take a water, thanks." When he noticed a couple more inches of her bare legs revealed as she reached down into the fridge, he forced himself to avert his gaze. A quick glance allowed him to view the entirety of her home—the living area and kitchen making up the main room, a door that led to a bathroom he was pretty sure he couldn't even fit in and a narrow staircase that led to a loft that served as her bedroom if the edge of the mattress he saw was any indication.

"So what do you think?" she asked as she handed him the cold bottle of water.

"It's…cozy."

"I know, right?" She surveyed her home with a satisfied look on her face.

"You really don't mind living in such a small space?"

"Nope. It's all I need for now."

"For now?"

"It's okay for a single person, but even I don't see fitting an entire family in here."

An entire family? Was she dating someone? And why on God's green earth did that thought irritate him? The miniature room seemed to shrink even more, their proximity to each other suddenly feeling awkward, and he had to forcibly keep himself from beating a retreat.

What the hell? That pigeon really had scrambled his brain.

He screwed the top off the water bottle with one quick motion and downed about half the contents.

Mandy laughed. "You must be as hot and thirsty as I am."

She had no idea how right she was. As if to make things even more uncomfortable, when she took her own drink he couldn't take his eyes off the column of her neck or the trickle of water that escaped and ran down it.

"Well, I better get going." Thankfully it only took him two strides to get from her living room to the front porch of her little dollhouse.

Mandy followed him out, closing the door behind her, no doubt to preserve the precious chilled air. "Thanks for bringing me home."

He descended the step and had started toward his truck but then he turned halfway back toward her. "Least I could do. I was the one who put your car out of commission." Then it hit him he was basically stranding her here alone with no mode of transportation. "How are you going to get back into town to work?"

"Maybe Devon can pick me up." She gestured toward the side of her tiny house. "Or I have a bike I can ride."

The idea of her trying to safely ride into town on a road with a nonexistent shoulder sent a big bolt of "nope" straight to his brain.

"You are not riding a bike on that road," he said. "You're liable to get taken out by a horse trailer or some fool driving too fast."

"You volunteering to be my chauffeur?" The little teasing smile on her face had him thinking he might do whatever she asked of him.

"Yeah. As a matter of fact, I am."

Her smile fell away in obvious surprise. "I was kidding, Ben."

"I know, but it's my fault you don't have your car, so I'll take you wherever you need to go until Greg can fix it."

"It's actually the pigeon's fault."

"Unless he's got a driver's license and a pigeon-mobile, you're stuck with me. When do you have to be at work next?"

"Um, eight in the morning."

"Then I'll see you at seven forty." He tapped two fingers to the edge of his hat in farewell then made for his truck before he could think too hard about why he'd just committed himself to who knew how much time away from his work.

As he started the truck and made the turn to leave, Mandy was still standing in the same spot looking every bit as surprised by the day's turn of events as he was.

Chapter Two

Mandy had just finished her salad and was enjoying a second glass of wine when her phone rang. She'd been so lost in her thoughts that the sound startled her, causing her to nearly slosh wine over the rim of her glass. That was just what she needed to end this day, to waste perfectly good cabernet.

The phone display showed it was her best friend, Devon, calling. "Hey."

"Are you okay? Cole said you were in an accident." Cole being Devon's superhot husband.

"I'm fine. I wasn't in an accident, though my car was."

"Huh?"

Mandy explained what had happened and that her car was currently sitting at Greg Bozeman's repair shop so he could assess the damage.

"Take whatever time off you need," Devon said.

"I don't need time off. I told you I'm perfectly fine."

"Well, okay. I'll pick you up in the morning, then."

"It's your day off. I'm sure you have sappy married-people things to do. Besides, I already have a ride."

"Oh, well, tell your mom I said hi. I need to swing by and see her soon."

Mandy considered letting Devon think her mother was the one chauffeuring her, but she was curious how her friend would react to the truth. Would it be no big deal? Or would her reaction validate how Mandy had sort of been freaking out since Ben made his offer and drove away with a promise to see her in the morning? She took a deep breath. Only one way to find out.

"Ben's actually going to be taking me to work."

"Feels guilty, huh?"

Okay, so no big deal. Mandy chalked up her overreaction to Ben's kindness to a long, tiring day and heat exhaustion. Oh, and the fact he was superhot.

"Yeah, I guess."

"What are you not saying?"

That was the problem with being friends with someone most of your life. They could even read your thoughts, no eye contact required.

"Nothing. I'm worn out and I've had some wine. I just need to go to bed and sleep today away."

"Do you know how to party on a Saturday night or what?"

"Not all of us have a sizzling-hot cowboy to get frisky with."

"Maybe you could," Devon said. "Last I heard, Ben was single. And you gotta admit he's not hard to look at."

She'd walked right into that one, hadn't she?

"I'll be sure to tell Cole you think so the next time I see him."

"Listen, chickie, I received no end of teasing from you about Cole, so it's my turn to dish it out."

"Good night, Devon." Mandy hung up and knew exactly how Devon would react the moment she did. They'd been through many similar scenarios since the moment they both acquired their first cell phones.

As if on cue, her phone buzzed with a text. With a sigh, she looked at the display.

You know you just confirmed you like Ben by hanging up on me, right?

Mandy took a swig of wine and texted back. Sorry, wrong number.

She imagined Devon laughing as she read the reply. Why hadn't she just let Devon think her mother was the one driving her?

Because there was a part of her, the part that inhabited all giggly teenage girls and evidently never went away, that wanted to talk about a boy she thought was cute. And Ben Hartley was way beyond cute. She leaned her head back and closed her eyes, picturing how he'd looked standing there next to her car, talking to Greg. Tall, lean, his blond hair peeking out from under his cowboy hat. Her body temperature had gone up more than even the scorching heat of the day could account for, and it did so again now just thinking about it. Even the blissfully cool interior of her home wasn't enough to prevent the flush to her skin.

Maybe this was all Devon's fault. After all, her best friend wore a permanent grin of satisfaction on her face these days. It was only natural to want a little of that for herself, right? And she could do worse than Ben Hartley. Not that he was even interested. They'd lived in the same town for as long as she could remember and they'd never been more than classmates as kids and passing acquaintances as adults. But couldn't the same be said about Devon and Cole? And look how that had turned out—wedded bliss.

Mandy shook that thought away. Ben was only going out of his way to help her because he felt responsible for the accident.

But a bit of fantasizing never hurt anybody, did it? No one ever needed to know what she thought about while sitting here in her own home enjoying her wine. Enjoying imagining what it might be like to kiss Ben Hartley.

OF COURSE HALF his family was outside and able to see his return in a truck more damaged than when he'd left earlier that afternoon. That was just how his day was going. And when he parked and got out of the truck, the amusement on his brother Adam's and sister Sloane's faces told him the pigeon story was already winging its way around the county.

"You're just in time for dinner," Sloane said. "We're having pigeon pie."

He moved quickly, grabbing her and tossing her over his shoulder and spinning her round and round.

Sloane banged on his back. "Put me down!"

He just laughed until the toe of her boot connected

with his thigh. That caused him to release her so quickly she stumbled and nearly fell when her feet hit the ground.

"Can't take a little teasing?" she asked.

"I've already had more than a little."

"You had to see this coming the moment that bird flew in your window," Adam said as he leaned against the front of his own truck.

Ben walked past his siblings. "Some days I wish Mom and Dad had adopted only one kid."

"That would have been me," Neil said as he appeared at the edge of the front porch, evidently on his way home to Arden.

Ben growled at his older brother as he shoved past him, as well, on his way inside. He'd retreat to his leather shop if he wasn't so hungry he was afraid he might eat one of the saddles he was making.

As soon as he stepped into the kitchen, his mom hurried over to him and clasped his chin in her fingers then turned his head sideways the same way she had when Billy Castner had given him a shiner in the sixth grade.

Ben took a step back from her. "I'm okay. It was just a little fender bender. Stop worrying."

She placed her hands on her hips and narrowed her eyes at him. "I'm your mother. It's what moms do. I swear, I thought I'd get you kids grown and you'd stop giving me gray hairs."

He tilted his head at that comment.

His mom held up a finger. "Not one word about how would I even be able to tell."

"I wouldn't dream of it."

She patted his cheek. "Smart boy."

He'd stopped being a boy a long time ago, but he loved his mom enough to let her call him whatever she wanted. She and his dad had saved him from a life of way worse than overzealous mothering, after all. Not that he'd made it easy for them.

Damn, that was the last thing he wanted to think about. He'd rather deal with jokes about head-butting a pigeon every day for the next year.

"Doesn't look like too much damage to your truck," his dad said as he entered the kitchen.

"No. Mandy's car got the worst of it."

"How bad?" his mom asked.

"It's crunched in the front. Probably the radiator is done for. Greg's looking at it."

Sloane snorted. "He'll probably charge her a few dates to pay for it."

Ben's jaw clenched at the thought of Greg with his hands all over Mandy. What in the—

"Nah," his youngest sister, Angel, said. "They already went out once. No spark."

"Really?" his mom said. "Mandy's such a pretty girl, and it's about time Greg stopped flitting around like a butterfly and settled down."

"Not everyone wants to get married and have two-point-five kids, Mom," Adam said.

Their mom ruffled Adam's thick, dark, wavy hair as she passed behind where he sat at the table. "They do when they find the right person. You'll see."

Ben disagreed in his mind but kept quiet. He'd never told anyone about his decision not to have a family. He knew it'd upset his mother especially, that she'd try to talk him out of it. Best just to avoid the topic altogether.

With the food on the table, they all settled into their places. All except Neil. Ben still hadn't quite gotten used to his older brother no longer living under the same roof. He was pleased for Neil and Arden—they'd both been through a lot and deserved to be happy. It was just odd to be the oldest sibling at the dinner table now.

"Did you know the Websters' place got subdivided?" he asked, steering the conversation away from settling down and producing heirs.

"I did hear that," his dad said. "Seems as if it'd be a mighty big headache dealing with lots of deals instead of just one."

"Mandy said they didn't want to sell to anyone like Franklin Evans." The man had thought the simple fact that he wanted the Rocking Heart was enough that Ben's parents would just up and sell a ranch that had been in the family nearly a century. Ben still smiled every time he thought about how Arden had put the self-important jerk in his place.

His dad chuckled. "I always did like Tom Webster."

"So Mandy bought part of it?" his mom asked, a little too much loaded curiosity in her tone.

"Yeah, couple of acres on the creek."

"She got one of those tiny houses, didn't she?" Sloane asked. "I saw them towing it through town some time back."

"Yeah, not much bigger than our doghouse."

"I think they're fascinating," Angel said.

"Not very practical, though."

Angel shrugged. "Depends on what you're looking for."

"You sound like Mandy," he said.

"That right?" There was no denying his mom's curious tone.

Sloane elbowed him in the ribs, not hard but enough to draw his attention. "Now that she's got Neil headed toward happily-ever-after, you know you're next, right?"

"Never heard a rule that said marriages had to go in birth order. Maybe you're next." He glanced down the table. "You'd like to be the mother of the bride, wouldn't you, Mom?"

This time the jab to the ribs was a bit more forceful.

"Indeed I would. And both of my girls will make beautiful brides."

"I'm going to kill you in your sleep," Sloane said under her breath to him.

He just smiled wide at her, grateful the conversation had veered away from him and Mandy. Not that there was a "him and Mandy."

But after dinner, his thoughts kept straying to her as he headed to his workshop to log some progress on a saddle he was making for a rancher over in Kimble County who'd seen the feature Arden had written on his custom saddles in the *Blue Falls Gazette*.

He couldn't stop thinking about how nice Mandy's legs had looked below that flowered skirt. How many times had he seen Mandy Richardson in his life? Even spoken to her? Dozens. Hundreds, probably. Why today, of all days, was he suddenly attracted to her?

He'd just finished tacking a circle of leather to the top of the saddle's horn when his phone rang. He tossed his hammer down on the workbench and pulled his phone from his back pocket. Greg Bozeman's name stared up at him. Why was Greg calling him?

"Hey, what's up?"

"You with Mandy?"

"No. I dropped her off at her place on the way home. Why?"

"I tried calling to talk to her about her car but got no answer. Thought you two might be together."

Ben rolled his eyes. "Nope. Try her again."

"Can't. Hot date tonight. Can you call and tell her it's going to be a few days before I can get her car fixed?"

"There's this thing now called voice mail."

"It was full. Couldn't leave a message."

"Fine, I'll tell her."

"Thanks. Gotta run." As the call ended, Ben couldn't help but wonder who in the world Greg was going out with. He had to have run through every eligible female in the Hill Country by now. The dude was either very careful or very lucky that he didn't have miniature versions of himself running over all of central Texas.

Ben shoved the phone back in his pocket and picked up a thick, circular piece of leather that would hide the nail heads. But as he made his way through the familiar successive steps—carving a groove around the top of the leather, punching holes around the edge for the stitching, and sewing the layers together—he couldn't help wondering why Mandy hadn't answered her phone.

Maybe she'd simply gone to sleep early. Or turned off her phone because she was just done with her rotten day. Possibly drunk herself into a stupor. Oh, hell, what if she'd wandered outside and fallen off that little porch and broken something? Or toddled down to the creek and ended up drowning in, like, a teaspoon of water.

What could it hurt to give her a call to pass on Greg's message? No, he wasn't calling just to make sure his suddenly overactive imagination wasn't correct and that she hadn't managed to meet her undignified end.

The phone rang three times before she finally picked up, sounding out of breath.

"You okay?"

She hesitated for a moment. "Ben?"

"Yeah. What have you been doing, pushing your little house to a new spot?"

"No, I was out trying to chase off what I swear was a mountain lion."

"What?"

"I saw it out the window. At first I thought maybe I'd just had too much wine, but then the thing turned and looked at me. I was feeling a little bit too much as if he was sizing me up for his dinner."

"So you went outside? I hope you had a gun."

"No, but I made an unholy racket with a couple of cooking pots. Good thing I don't have close neighbors."

"You did have too much wine if you went outside without protection. Good Lord, woman. I'll be right there."

"It's gone now."

"Yeah, I'm coming anyway. Do not go back outside."

"Huh. You always this bossy?"

"When the occasion calls for it."

His parents, Angel and his niece, Julia, looked up when he burst into the house less than a minute later. When he unlocked the gun cabinet and pulled out his rifle, his dad stood, probably thinking there was some danger to their cattle herd. If Mandy really had seen a mountain lion, there very well could be.

"Going to Mandy's. She says she saw a mountain lion outside her house."

"Oh, be careful," his mom said as she scooted to the edge of the couch.

"I'll go with you," his dad said.

"No, it's okay. The thing's probably gone by now. Just want to make sure. You might want to check that the animals are secure here, though."

His dad gave him a nod.

"I'll give you a hand," Adam said to their dad as he walked into the room.

"If you don't think Mandy will be safe there, you bring her back here." This time, there was no teasing in his mom's voice, telling him that her chief concern was Mandy's safety, not his dating life.

On the drive to Mandy's, he watched for any signs of the big cat along the sides of the road but saw only a deer bound into the trees and a dead armadillo belly-up on the narrow gravel shoulder.

When he turned into Mandy's driveway, the lights from her little house were like a beacon in the surrounding darkness. He slowed and scanned the entire area illuminated by his headlights. As he pulled up next to her house, Mandy stepped out onto the small porch. The moment he got a full view of her, he forgot about the mountain lion. She'd changed into skimpy little pajama shorts and a matching orange top with thin lacy straps.

This day was trying its damnedest to kill him.

The reason for his visit came crashing back into his mind, and he hurried out of the truck and motioned her inside.

"I'll check around, see if your visitor's gone."

She ignored him and continued to stand on the porch as he pulled his rifle out of the gun rack in the back window.

"I'd feel a lot better if you went inside," he said.

"Well, I'd feel a lot better if you didn't go poking around in the dark looking for the big kitty cat."

He did a mental eye roll as he scanned the area, hoping she'd just imagined seeing a mountain lion. She'd been drinking wine, after all. But she didn't seem overly intoxicated, so he took the possibility of the predator seriously. It wasn't until he reached the slope that led down to the creek that he got confirmation she hadn't been imagining the cat.

He glanced back at where she stood, the porch light putting her in silhouette. Using his flashlight, he looked beyond the reach of the truck's headlights and the illumination coming from her little house. He didn't see any eyes shining back at him, but that didn't mean the animal wasn't lurking nearby. He'd report the sighting to Parks and Wildlife in the morning and spread the word to other area residents. Ranchers would need to keep an eye on their animals, and anyone with small children and pets needed to be alert, as well.

He took a few steps backward, ready to raise the rifle if necessary, before turning and walking toward Mandy.

"See anything?"

Ben did his best to keep his eyes fixed on her face, but it was damned hard not to let his gaze drift downward. Those little pajama shorts made her legs look a mile long even though she was only of average height. For a really ill-advised moment he imagined running his hands up all that bare skin.

Remembering she'd asked him a question, he said, "Tracks down by the creek. Mom suggested you come stay at our place tonight."

Mandy's eyes widened a little and she glanced toward the creek. "That's not necessary. He didn't bother me before, just scared the daylights out of me."

"No guarantee he won't come back."

"I'll just stay inside."

Ben put one foot up on the single porch step and extended the gun toward her. "Then I want you to keep this here tonight just in case."

She was shaking her head before he even finished speaking. "I won't use that. I doubt the mountain lion is going to open the door and stroll inside. Besides, I'd be more likely to shoot off my own foot."

With a sigh of frustration, he turned and sank down onto the edge of the porch.

"What are you doing?"

"If you won't do anything to protect yourself, guess I'll have to do it for you."

When he heard her exhale in exasperation, he didn't know whether to laugh or brace for a frying pan upside his head.

Chapter Three

Mandy stared at the back of Ben's head. "You know you're being ridiculous, right?"

"You don't seem overly concerned that a mountain lion walked across your front yard. You don't even have a vehicle here in case something happened."

"I figure if he didn't try to eat me after hearing me squeal at the sight of him out the window or when I made all that racket with the pots, I'm safe. He probably hightailed it away from the crazy lady."

"Maybe." He didn't sound terribly convinced.

"You're not seriously going to sit there all night, are you?" She wouldn't get one wink of sleep. Of course, after seeing a mountain lion only a few yards away, she doubted she would anyway. But Ben didn't need to know that.

"I don't feel comfortable leaving you alone, especially since it's my fault you're stranded here," he said.

"If I consent to keeping the gun here, will you stop worrying?"

"I'd feel better."

"Fine, then. Now, I'm sure you have better things to do than sit on my front porch and stare at nothing."

A long moment passed before he said anything. "I'll leave in a bit."

As he continued to scan the darkness surrounding her home, Mandy wondered when she'd ever had such an insane day. The ringing of her phone drew her back inside. This time it was her mom.

"Hey, Mom."

"Hi, hon. Wanted to make sure you got home okay."

"Yeah, Ben dropped me off on his way home." She wasn't about to tell her mom he was currently playing sentry on her front porch because she'd seen a mountain lion lurking about. Her mom would be out here in no time, despite the fact she needed to go to sleep soon in order to be up early for work. Mandy had planned to talk to her mom tonight about cutting back her hours, but it was a conversation best had in person.

"Have you heard how bad the car is?"

"Not yet." Even if she had, she wasn't going to divulge those details either and give her mom something else to worry about. "It's not too bad, though."

"I'm more than happy to come get you in the morning."

"Mom, it's taken care of. You don't need to worry about me, okay? I'm a big girl—have been for a long time."

Her mom laughed a little. "Old habits die hard, I guess. Well, I'll let you get back to whatever you were doing. Have a good night, hon."

"You, too. Love you."

Her mom reciprocated the sentiment then hung up. No doubt she was tired from another day of cleaning rooms at the Wildflower Inn followed by a shift as a dishwasher at a café over in Fredericksburg.

Mandy placed her phone back on the countertop and stared at it for several seconds before glancing toward the porch. She could barely see the top of Ben's head through the glass in the front door. She wanted nothing more than to crawl into bed and put an end to a day filled with one frustration after another. She was normally a cheerful person, and she hated feeling irritated at every turn.

She closed her eyes and took a slow, deep breath, then let it out just as slowly. It was still within her power to make something positive out of what was left of the day. She should just do that in something other than her skimpy summer pajamas. She wasn't even wearing a bra!

After hurriedly pulling on a T-shirt and gym shorts, and replacing the bra she'd ditched about five seconds after Ben left earlier, she grabbed a couple of bottles of water from the fridge and went back outside. She plunked herself down beside Ben and extended a bottle toward him.

"Figured if you were going to sit out here, you at least should have something cold to drink."

He took the bottle. "Thanks. And sorry if I came across as bossy. Been one of those days."

She smiled. "Yeah, I know."

A grin tugged at the edge of his mouth, and that small change in his expression made her middle feel funny. Not funny as in ha-ha or "I'm going to be sick," but rather "Oh, that's a nice hint of a smile on a really nice face. I wonder what those lips would feel like on mine."

Yep, she'd officially gone bonkers.

"Guess we both could use a do-over," he said.

"My mom has always said if you're having a bad day, don't focus on it. Just remember there's a brand-new one coming in a few hours."

"Your mom sounds very Zen."

"Just practical. She doesn't see the point in wallowing in self-pity. Chances are it won't change anything and will only make you feel worse."

"If life gives you lemons, make lemonade?"

"Oh, great. Now I want, like, a bucket of lemonade."

"I'm not sure you have room for a bucket in there," Ben said, gesturing over his shoulder with his thumb.

"That's it. It's now my mission to make you a tiny-house fan."

He shook his head and chuckled as if she was setting herself up for a Sisyphean task.

"Was that Greg calling again?"

Again? "No, my mom."

"Guess I didn't get to that part earlier. Greg called and said that it would be a few days until he could fit your car into his schedule."

She sighed. "Well, that's about par for today. Why didn't he call me instead?"

"He said he did, that you didn't answer and that your voice mail was full."

Mandy's forehead wrinkled. "No, it's not. And there were no missed calls."

Ben shook his head.

"Let me guess. Greg is messing with us."

He nodded. "Guess he got infected with the matchmaking virus that seems to be spreading all over town."

"You say that as if it's the bubonic plague."

"At least people don't go around trying to give you the plague."

"Wow, remind me to tell the single ladies of Blue Falls to give you a wide berth."

"And there went my dating life, pitiful as it is."

Mandy laughed. Who knew Ben Hartley was so funny? And dang if being funny wasn't one of the things that really attracted her to a guy.

"We should totally mess with Greg, convince him he's the best matchmaker ever. Go in tomorrow and tell him we've set a date. I could take a bridal magazine and ask him to help me pick out a dress."

"I'll ask him to be my best man."

"Oh, oh, I've got it! Tell him we want him to get ordained online so he can marry us."

Ben snorted. "Greg Bozeman an ordained minister. And that's where you lost me."

"Yeah, that was the step no one would actually believe." She stared out into the darkness. "We could always toilet-paper his house as payback."

"Shrink-wrap his truck."

"No, wrap it in pink streamers. We just happen to have a couple of cases in the back of the shop."

Ben slowly turned his head to look at her, and up this

close, even in the half-light, his blue eyes threatened to make off like a bandit with her ability to breathe.

"Already stocking up on decorations for Valentine's Day?"

Valentine's Day. Romance. Kisses in the moonlight.

Oops, keep your brain in the present if you don't want to look like a dimwit.

"No. They were delivered to the wrong place. Were supposed to go to a party store in Austin."

"That mix-up doesn't make sense."

"Nope, but the company said to just keep them and they'd send new ones to the right address." She smiled wide. "I'm thinking that's the universe telling us they have a greater purpose here in Blue Falls."

He lifted a dark blond brow. "You're serious?"

"I am."

"And if we get caught?"

"We won't."

"You know this is going on the front page of the *Gazette* if we do," he said.

"I expect you to use your connection at the paper to keep that from happening."

He chuckled and shook his head. "What the hell? Not as if I'm going to get any work done tonight anyway."

"And it'll be a lot more fun than sitting out here waiting for Mr. Kitty to make an appearance."

"Mr. Kitty?"

"Makes him seem less scary." She jumped to her feet. "Be right back."

Mandy hurried inside and pulled on her sneakers, trying not to think about how excited she was to go out pranking with Ben. Or how the idea of it seemed to dispel her earlier fatigue and frustration. She didn't dawdle, not wanting him to have second thoughts. Maybe she should let him go home. Maybe she could ignore how much she liked being around him. But she simply didn't want to.

He looked up at her approach. "We're really doing this?"

"Come on. Live a little."

She expected him to call a halt to her crazy plan, but when he didn't, she nearly sprinted to his truck. Granted, that probably wasn't the wisest move when a mountain lion could be lurking about. She'd probably just made herself look even more like dinner. But she made it safely and breathed in a quick, deep inhalation while Ben took one more look at the surrounding area before opening his door.

His truck smelled like him—a mixture of horses, leather and another striking scent that reminded her of pine trees and long, tall Texans making Wranglers the sexiest piece of clothing on the planet.

Ben secured the rifle in the rack in the back window then slid into the driver's seat. "I must be crazy doing this."

"Sometimes you need a little crazy in your life to make things interesting."

As Ben turned the truck around and headed down her driveway, she watched his hands on the steering wheel. They looked strong, probably also a little rough from his work on the family ranch. She really needed to find a safe topic of conversation before he caught her staring or, heaven forbid, drooling. Maybe she ought to toilet-paper Devon's house instead for putting these kinds of hot-and-bothered thoughts in her head in the first place.

"So, did Greg happen to say what all he was going to have to fix on my car?"

"No, just that it would take a few days."

"Well, that's frustratingly vague."

"Just part of the frustrating theme of the day."

"It wasn't all bad."

Ben glanced across the cab at her. "Which part exactly didn't make you want to crawl under the covers and start over tomorrow?"

Now, why had he gone and mentioned crawling under the covers? Images that had no place taking up residence in her head strolled right in and made themselves at home.

"Let's see. I may have been on my feet all day, but at least I have a job." She held up two fingers. "I did have some nice wine before my feline scare." She pointed out the windshield at the road in front of them. "And this will be fun. I haven't done anything like this since high school. Oh, but don't tell my mother that. I don't want her image of me as the perfect child to be shattered."

He chuckled. "I doubt my mom thinks of me as the perfect child."

"I was under the impression you and your mom have a good relationship."

"We do. There's no doubt she loves me. She's just not blind."

"My mom isn't blind," she said with mock offense.

He looked over at her, eyebrow raised. "Uh-huh."

Mandy playfully swatted his upper arm with the backs of her fingers, which just made him laugh even more.

When they rolled into town, she directed him to the alley behind the strip of stores along Main Street. He parked outside the back door of A Good Yarn. She fumbled with her ring of keys when he stepped up behind her. She'd swear she could feel his warm breath on her neck and wondered what would happen if she turned to face him.

Oh, get a grip on your hormones, woman.

She managed to finally slip the right key into the lock. A rush of cool air wafted over her when she opened the door. She flicked on the light to the storage room just inside the door and Ben entered behind her.

"You'd think we live in North Dakota judging by how much yarn you've got here."

She noticed him eyeing the shelves of brightly colored yarns stretching up one wall. "Knitting is enjoying a resurgence in popularity."

"It must be, to support a store in a town this size."

"We have other things, too." She pointed toward the shelves filled with bolts of cloth, sewing notions, candles, soaps and a variety of other craft items. "And tourism is growing by leaps and bounds, which really helps."

He nodded. "I've gotten a bit more work because of the rodeos."

"Saddles, right? I saw the article Arden did about them."

"Yeah."

Realization hit her. “That’s what you were going to work on tonight, isn’t it? I’m sorry. I get myself caught up in stuff sometimes.”

“It’s okay. The way today has gone, I would’ve probably just nailed my thumb to the saddle anyway. Or cut it off.”

“So I’m actually performing a service, then, saving you from yourself.”

He huffed out a laugh. “Where were you when that pigeon attacked me?”

“I can’t be everywhere at once.” She kicked one of the boxes that contained the streamers. “Let’s usher this day out on a fun note.”

MANDY WAS RIGHT. Turning Greg’s truck into what looked like a pickup-shaped piece of cotton candy was just what he needed to lift his mood. The only problem was he was having a hard time not cracking up. From the light in Mandy’s eyes and the way she kept having to cover her mouth, it appeared she was having the same problem. When she snorted after tying a big pink bow on the truck’s trailer hitch, he nearly lost it.

“You know, this can also be a long-time-coming payback for when Greg got me in trouble in high school. He hung those pictures of swimsuit models all over the school and put Mr. Kushner’s face on them, then swore up and down that I did it.”

“I remember that. It was hilarious. Well, not that you got in trouble if he did it.”

“Oh, he did it, all right.”

“Why didn’t you tell everyone it was him?”

"Let's just say it was better to take the heat for that than deny it."

"That sounds as if he had something on you."

Ben shrugged. "Maybe."

"You know I'm going to bug you until you tell me, so you might as well go ahead."

"It was a long time ago. Not relevant anymore."

Mandy shook her finger at him "Oh, no you don't. You can't start that story and not finish it."

Why had he opened his mouth?

Mandy shoved his shoulder in a playful gesture matched by the mischievous grin she wore. The sudden urge to kiss that grin right off her mouth challenged his willpower not to act on that thought.

"Come on. Fess up."

He used the last of his roll of streamer to completely cover the driver's side mirror. "I had a thing for Shantele Drayton, but I knew I didn't have a chance so didn't want her to know. The only reason Greg knew is I let it slip one night when a bunch of us were out camping. Luckily no one else heard me."

When Mandy didn't respond, he glanced toward her and found her staring at where she'd managed to cover the rear tire in pink. He got the impression, though, that she was staring instead at a memory.

"Mandy?"

"I think that about does it." She took a step back and admired their handiwork.

The mood had changed, and he had no idea why.

"You okay?"

"Yep."

"Uh-huh." He didn't think he'd ever heard anything less convincing. It must have shown on his face, too.

"Fine. I just think Shantele was a self-centered twit. Every time she found out somebody wanted something or liked someone else, she either took it for herself or spilled the beans."

"You sound as if you're speaking from experience."

"It's possible."

"And that experience would be...?"

Mandy propped her hands on her hips. "If you must know, Devon and I were shopping for homecoming our freshman year and there was a dress I really wanted. But I had to save up to buy it. The lady who owned the store agreed to set it aside for me for a week until I got my babysitting money. When I went back to get it, not only had Shantele bought it, she was wearing it out of the store as she walked by me. She'd been in the store that first day and overheard Devon and me talking about the dress."

"But the lady said she'd save it for you."

"The dress was on sale, but Shantele offered her full price. Money talks. Devon was so mad because she could have bought it for me, but I wouldn't let her."

"Did Shantele have something against you?"

"I won the spelling bee in third grade and she came in second."

"You think she held a grudge that long? Over a spelling bee?"

"She's probably still walking around now with that grudge. Shantele is used to getting what she wants. But I smile every time I hear the word *tantrum*. Kind of appropriate that she couldn't spell it. So I personally think you were better off without her."

"Sounds as if you're probably right. I never said teenage boys were smart."

Mandy laughed at that, then pulled out her phone and aimed it at the truck. "This would be better in the daylight, but I've got to at least try to take this for posterity's sake."

When she snapped the photo, it felt as if the flash lit up half of Blue Falls. And moments later, Greg's front porch light came on.

"Oh, crap!" Mandy said as she fumbled her phone, nearly dropping it.

A shot of adrenaline mixed with laughter went through Ben as he grabbed Mandy's hand and pulled her away from the truck. "Come on."

Mandy squealed then laughed as she kept pace with him. The sudden appearance of headlights caused her to yelp. He switched their direction and pulled her into a darkened area on the opposite side of Greg's garage, which sat a short distance from his house, surrounded by cars in need of repair—including Mandy's.

They were both breathing heavily, but the sound of Greg's surprised "What the…?" was still clear and caused Mandy to descend into a fit of giggles.

"Shh or you're going to get us caught."

When she dropped her forehead against his chest, his breathing screeched to a halt. He resisted the urge to place his hand against her back to bring her closer. Instead, he smiled as he felt the laughter shaking her body.

"I'll find out who you are!" Greg called out, which only made Mandy shake harder with suppressed laughter.

"Cut it out," Ben whispered close to her ear, trying to ignore the flowery smell of her. "You're going to make me lose it, too."

"Sorry," she whispered as she looked up.

Her laughter froze when their eyes met. The brightness staring back at him stole what was left of his breath. And from the way she was gazing up at him, he knew he wasn't alone.

Chapter Four

Come on, lungs, breathe!

Honestly, how could someone forget how to breathe? But as Mandy looked up at Ben's face, it was as if someone had flipped the switch on her respiratory system to Off.

Damn, he was even more handsome up close. Thank goodness they were in near darkness. If he looked this good hiding in the shadows, this type of proximity in full light might just be her end. His mouth parted, and she felt her traitorous body start to move toward him.

But the sudden sound of footsteps on gravel caused them both to jump. Ben's arms came around her and pulled her even deeper into the shadows. Greg might very well be about to find them, but all she could think about was the warmth and weight of Ben's palms against her back, the faint smell of laundry detergent clinging to his shirt even after a long, hot day. The way her breasts were pressed against his chest and how much she liked how that felt and wasn't in any hurry to end the contact.

It seemed to take forever for Greg to give up with a muttered curse and head back toward his house. That he hadn't looked in just the right spot to see them was no small miracle. Ben didn't move until the sound of Greg's footsteps totally faded. When he did, part of her wanted to whimper.

But he only eased his hold on her, not totally releasing her.

"That was close," he said.

"It was." Every part of her wanted him to kiss her. Before that afternoon, she couldn't even say when she'd last had a passing thought about Ben Hartley. Now she was having thoughts that would make the knitting club that met at A Good Yarn blush. Or maybe they'd remember their own youth and cheer her on. Was she daring enough to steal that kiss herself? She was just beginning to lift onto her toes when Ben set her farther away and stepped out of the nook where they'd hidden.

"We better get out of here while the getting's good."

He didn't take her hand, and she had a ridiculously hard time not reaching for his. That was it—she needed to go home and get a good night's sleep. Maybe she'd wake up and not feel on the edge of throwing caution to whatever wind happened to blow by.

They stayed quiet as they walked back to where he'd parked his truck. She opened her door and hopped in before he could open it for her. Best to leave her sudden attraction to Ben back there in their dark hiding place. If he wasn't interested, she sure didn't want to make a complete fool of herself. Not in a town the size of Blue Falls, anyway. Somehow someone would be able to read the truth on her face and she'd never hear the end of it. Worse, town matchmaker Verona Charles would move the potential pairing to the top of her matchmaking list regardless of Mandy's or Ben's feelings about getting together.

When the quiet stretched too long for her comfort, she said, "Well, I think the streamer antics have finally worn me out. I'll probably conk out before my head hits the pillow."

"Looking forward to some sleep myself." He didn't even glance toward her and sounded more distant than he had a few minutes before.

Maybe he was simply as tired as she was, but it was also possible that he was concerned she'd felt more in that up-close-and-personal moment than he had and perhaps expected something from him. She didn't force any further conversation, instead leaning her head back against the seat and staring out the window. Before the lights of Blue Falls even faded into the darkness of ranch country, she felt herself drifting and her eyelids drooping.

MANDY JERKED AWAKE when something shook her. Had she been having a bad dream? About to fall out of bed? Movement out of the corner of her eye startled her so much that she jumped and in the process banged her elbow.

"Ow!" She rubbed the offended body part as the truth settled in her mind. "Oh, jeez, I fell asleep?"

"Vandalism is tiring." Ben smiled a little, relieving the awkwardness that had settled between them as they'd left town.

"Yep. That excursion will probably last me another

decade. Thanks for taking part in my temporary insanity."

"I'm blaming the pigeon."

She laughed. "That excuse expires at midnight."

"I'm going to expire before then."

"Me, too," she said as she clasped the door handle. "Good night, Ben."

"Wait."

Her heart leaped, but then she saw him reaching for the rifle.

"I'll walk you to the door."

That sounded very chivalrous. Part of her wished it had romantic overtones, but she'd picked up enough of who Ben was in the last several hours to know it was instead his need to make sure she was safe before he left. Of course, that was nice in and of itself. She needed to focus on that and not on the part of her that was disappointed.

They walked side by side up to the porch. When she passed her frog statue, she thought about how he wasn't who she wanted to kiss tonight. Just a few more minutes and she'd be safely inside her house, away from her sudden abandonment of good sense. One didn't end the day by kissing the person who wrecked your car earlier in the day, especially when you'd known that person forever and would likely know them the rest of forever.

"You know how to use this?" he asked.

She eyed the rifle. "Only in the vaguest of terms."

Somehow she managed to pay attention to the instructions, enough that she was confident she wouldn't, in fact, shoot off her foot. That had to be an A plus for effort, considering how much her senses were demanding she ignore his actual words and instead focus on the warmth coming off his body, his undeniably male scent, the deep rumble of his voice, the memory of how it had felt to be pressed close to him with his strong arms around her.

"Got it," she said too suddenly, judging by the startled look on Ben's face. "Sorry, but Cinderella is about to turn back into a pumpkin."

"I know I'm a guy, but I'm pretty sure Cinderella wasn't the one who turned into a pumpkin."

"Whatever—it sounded better than 'poorly dressed, mistreated orphan girl.'"

Ben's amused smile caused a fluttery feeling inside her, as if she'd swallowed a migration of butterflies who'd taken up square dancing.

"I'll see you in the morning," he said.

"Yep."

Yep? Really? She supposed that was better than the other thought that had been near the tip of her tongue—that he might as well stay over since it was only a few hours before he had to be back here. Instead, she gave him a nod and stepped inside the house. She resisted the urge to bang her head against the wall, instead storing the gun safely in the corner.

She finally let out a long breath and sank onto the couch when she heard Ben start his truck. As the sound of the engine retreated into the night, an aloneness she'd never felt since moving to her own piece of land descended. The night surrounding her tiny house seemed darker, quieter, more filled with potential danger.

How could she feel so different from when she'd gotten up that morning? She was the same person with the same job, the same home. And yet as she sat there, there was no denying that something had changed within her sometime since she'd looked up at the sound of her car being crunched.

And she wasn't sure what she was going to do about it.

When Ben reached the porch of his family's home, his sisters were sitting in two of the rocking chairs in the dark.

"Thought maybe the mountain lion had eaten you," Sloane said.

He leaned against one of the porch supports. "Glad to see you were so concerned you decided to lounge out here with a glass of lemonade."

"What? I've got two other brothers."

"Sloane!" Angel said and kicked at her older sister's foot.

"What? He knows I'm just giving him a hard time." Sloane looked over at him. "Seriously, though, did you find the mountain lion? I'm not about to bring any more kids out here to camp in tents if it's still running around."

"I didn't see him, but there were tracks. He's not a small animal."

"Did you follow the tracks in the dark?"

He shook his head.

"Then where have you been all this time?" The teasing crept back into Sloane's voice.

He considered brushing off her question, but that would just make her more persistent, like a dang mosquito buzzing around his ear, determined to draw blood. Better to tell her the truth. Well, partial truth. He wasn't about to tell anyone about his unexpected reaction to Mandy, how he'd dang near kissed her as they'd hidden from Greg. She'd felt so good in his arms. Warm, soft, full of a zest for life.

"You remember that time Greg got me in trouble in high school?"

"How could I forget? Those pictures were epic. I thought Mr. Kushner was going to pop a vein."

"Mandy may have given me a way to finally get some payback."

"Okay, now I'm intrigued," Sloane said.

He told them about the wrongfully delivered pink streamers and how Mandy had suggested they wrap Greg's truck in them and how he, in an evident moment of insanity, went along with it. He mentioned how they'd almost been caught but skipped right over how he'd held Mandy in the dark, feeling her soft curves and her chest rising and falling against his, how he'd experienced the almost irresistible urge to drop his mouth to hers.

"I'd give good money to have seen Greg's face when he saw that truck," Sloane said.

"Heck, I'd settle just for seeing the truck." Angel laughed.

Ben pulled out his phone and scrolled to the photo Mandy had sent him then extended the phone to Angel.

"Oh, my, that's awesome," she said before handing the phone to Sloane.

Sloane snorted. "I cannot wait to tease Greg about this."

"Don't tell him who did it."

"I won't, but probably half the town knows about this by now. People are probably hopping in their cars to cruise by to see it."

"He may have it all off by now."

"Trust me, a fair number of people would have gone to gawk before he managed to remove all that. You and Mandy did an excellent job." She shook her head then looked up at him. "One thing I don't understand, though. How did that prank on Mr. Kushner even come up in conversation?"

He shrugged as he took his phone back. "Don't remember how we got on that topic."

"Nice try but you're lying."

"No, I'm not."

"Yep, you are, and I'm going to figure out what you're hiding."

"You live to annoy people, don't you?"

"Side benefit of being part of a big family."

He shook his head in annoyance. "Good night, Angel."

Sloane just laughed as he headed inside. He wished he'd gone straight in when he arrived instead of confessing what he'd been out doing. This day just needed to end before the house caved in on him.

MANDY DRANK THE last bit of coffee in her cup as she stared out the window over her sink, which gave her a good view of the driveway. She wasn't normally an anxious person, but waiting for Ben to arrive had her fidgety. She'd only been able to eat a piece of toast. There was probably a trip to Mehlerhaus Bakery in her future about midmorning.

She recognized how crazy it was to have a fear of morning-after awkwardness when it really wasn't a morning after. There'd been no sex. Not even any nakedness.

No! She did not need to think about Ben and being naked. Not when he would be arriving any minute.

It had taken her forever to fall asleep the night before, but she'd had the hope that she'd wake up and feel perfectly normal this morning. That all the unexpected attraction to Ben had simply been an odd side effect of the crazy day before she'd had. Ha! The attraction had followed her into sleep, where she'd had dreams about things that could have happened in that darkened corner next to Greg's shop if he hadn't come close to discovering her and Ben.

Mandy's face flushed and she splashed it with water for the umpteenth time that morning. Good thing she was a minimalist when it came to makeup—it only took her about thirty seconds to reapply it.

The sound of Ben's truck sent her heart into overdrive. That was it. She would call Greg when she got to work and tell him she needed her repaired car, like, yesterday.

She dumped the last dribbles of coffee into the sink, rinsed the cup and placed it on the counter. After a deep, calming breath, she grabbed her purse and headed outside. She didn't give him time to get out of his truck, stepping up to the passenger door as soon as he came to a stop.

"Good morning," she said with perhaps too much enthusiasm as she pulled herself up into the truck.

Ben looked across the cab at her, the area between his brows furrowed. "You always this peppy in the morning? If so, I'm going to have to rethink my offer to drive you to work."

"Grumpus."

He just growled at her and proceeded to back out of the driveway.

"I appreciate you taking me to work. You won't have to again. I'm calling Greg today to tell him I really need my car back."

"I don't mind," Ben said as he pulled out onto the road. "I just didn't sleep well."

A pang of guilt hit her. "I'm sorry I dragged you out last night."

"No need to apologize. It was actually the best part of my day."

The guilt in her middle got shoved aside by a zing of excitement. Acting normal would be so much easier if he didn't say things like that, even if he didn't mean it in the way she'd like him to.

"Admittedly, it only had to clear a really low bar," she said.

"True. Still, I wish I could have been a fly on the wall—or in the tree, I guess—while he was removing all those streamers."

Mandy smiled at that image in her mind. "Heaven help us if he finds out we did it."

She fidgeted when the conversation died. Normally, she didn't have trouble chatting away with people whether they were friends, casual acquaintances or complete strangers. But the buzzy feeling she'd gotten around Ben since the previous day had her second-guessing everything she might say. The fact that it was still hanging around this morning after a night of sleep and several hours away from him had her feeling equal parts antsy, thrilled and confused. How could you go basically your whole life knowing someone without feeling more than a passing knowledge that he was good-looking and then one day, whammo, your heart rate refused to behave itself around him?

"See the mountain lion again?"

Oh, good, safe topic.

"No. Hopefully he's moved on."

"Would be better if he's found before he hurts someone or attacks a pet or cattle."

"Will he be killed? That doesn't seem fair."

Ben glanced toward her. "If he's not hurt anyone, he may be relocated."

"Let's hope that happens." She wondered if Ben thought she was too much of a softy toward a wild animal, but she couldn't help it. The cat was just being a cat in a world where the ability to do so was shrinking every day. She didn't want anyone hurt or, heaven forbid, anything worse to happen, but she also didn't want the mountain lion put down just for scaring the daylights out of her by strolling across her yard.

Their trip into town seemed both too quick and glacially slow. She liked being around Ben, surprising as that might be, but his proximity also threw her off-kilter. A day of work and talking with people who weren't Ben Hartley might be what she needed to settle back into the normality that existed prior to his unfortunate bird to the head the day before.

He pulled into a spot a couple of doors down from A Good Yarn but left his truck running, indicating he had work to get back to.

"Thanks for the ride. Don't worry about picking me up."

"Until your car is fixed, you're just going to have to get used to me being your chauffeur."

Why was he being so adamant about that? "You sure are stubborn."

"So my mom has always said."

As she hopped out of his truck onto the sidewalk, she spotted a few familiar faces noticing whose vehicle she was exiting. Not that the entire town didn't already know he'd driven her home the day before. That was how things worked in small towns. Honestly, she and Ben would be lucky if the fact they were behind the Great Streamer Caper didn't become public knowledge.

"Happy saddle making," she said with a wave.

"Happy yarn selling."

Knowing that eyes were upon her, she made sure she didn't smile too widely and resisted the urge to watch him drive away. Instead, she unlocked the front door of the shop, walked inside and went straight to the phone.

It took Greg four rings to answer his phone at the garage. She supposed his office help hadn't arrived yet.

"Hey, it's Mandy Richardson. Just checking on my car."

"I've got a couple more in front of it, but I should be able to begin work on it tomorrow."

"Begin? How long is it going to take?"

Mandy paced the length of the three aisles lined with knitting, sewing and assorted craft supplies. "There's no way you can get to it sooner, like today?"

"I thought you had a driver for a while."

She detected the hint of teasing in his voice, and she had to bite her tongue to not ask him how he liked having a pink truck complete with a big bow.

"Ben has work to do. So do I. Work that is located nowhere near each other."

"Seems only fair. He was the one who ran into your car."

"Greg, I don't know if Verona Charles is paying you or something, but cut it out."

"What? I don't know what you're talking about."

"Bull. How about you stick to fixing cars—like mine?"

Mandy spotted Devon at the front of the shop. She hadn't even heard her come in and wondered how much of the conversation she'd heard. The way Mandy had urged her to go for Cole, she didn't have any doubt what her best friend would say when she found out that Mandy was attracted to Ben. After all, Devon would no doubt see some parallels since she'd known Cole for years without them spending any significant time together.

"I'll do what I can," Greg said in her ear.

She mumbled a quick thanks and hurried to hang up the phone. "Hey," she called out as she walked toward the front of the store. "What are you doing here?"

Devon shrugged. "Just decided to come in for a little bit."

Yeah, right.

Devon leaned her hip against the front of the counter that held the cash register, a grin rivaling the brightness of her red hair. "So, Ben Hartley, huh?"

Mandy pulled out her best Meryl Streep. "What about him?"

"Nice try." Devon motioned back down the aisle. "I heard you giving Greg an earful over your car. That is not the laid-back Mandy Richardson I know. So I asked myself, 'Self, why would she be in such a hurry to be free of her hunky chauffeur? Might it be because she's attracted to him and it's freaking her out?'"

Mandy snarled at her friend and walked past her to place the phone in the base charger. "Sometimes you're really annoying."

Devon laughed. "I think I might have said something very similar to you not all that long ago."

Mandy sank onto the tall stool behind the counter. "I feel as if I was the one hit in the head by the pigeon."

Devon turned to face her. "Why?"

Because she knew her friend would pry every bit of information out of her anyway, Mandy shared everything that had happened the previous day from the moment Ben had run into her car.

"I thought maybe I was having these weird feelings because it had been a crazy day or as a result of being around my besotted best friend all the time, that it would go away with a good night's sleep."

"But it didn't."

"Nope."

"And why is that a problem?"

Mandy shrugged. "I don't know. Just feels strange to suddenly start liking someone like this when I've known him forever, and not even been close friends."

"That sounds familiar."

"Trust me when I say I recognize the irony."

"Just go with it and see where it leads."

"What if it goes nowhere?"

"Then at least you'll know."

Was her attraction a temporary condition? If not, she didn't look forward to harboring it knowing that Ben wasn't interested. That sounded like a barrel of fun when they'd no doubt be unable to avoid each other for the rest of their lives. And what if he got married and started having a bunch of little miniature versions of himself?

Dang, her imagination was revved up on rocket fuel.

Devon's phone buzzed with a text. When she looked down at it, she laughed. "Looks as if your handiwork is making the rounds."

Mandy looked at the image of Greg's pink streamer-covered truck from the night before and noticed several people in the background with amused looks on their faces. She couldn't help a snort of her own laughter at the sight of that big pink bow on the trailer hitch.

"He'll probably spin this so that it actually was perpetrated by some gal who is madly in love with him," Mandy said.

"Why Verona hasn't set her sights on him yet, I have no idea. Maybe we should put a bug in her ear."

Mandy pointed toward the image on Devon's phone. "That might be the bug right there."

As the next couple of hours progressed, she threw herself into work while trying to forget about Ben and her unexpected attraction. But her brain was having none of it and kept thinking about his smile, his laugh, the feel of his arms around her as they'd hidden from Greg, how quickly he'd come to her front door when he thought she might be in danger from that mountain lion and how willing he'd been to take part in pranking Greg even after a long, tiring day. Damn, the man hit all her buttons, but now she understood why Devon had been so worried about confessing her true feelings to Cole. She couldn't imagine the awkwardness of repeatedly having to see the person you liked who didn't like you back. She suspected unrequited crushes didn't get any easier with age.

But would it be unrequited? Her attraction wasn't the only thing that had surprised her in the past twenty-four hours. The fact that she was so nervous about it, the possibility that it might not fade, and that she might find out Ben didn't want to explore that path with her had her feeling as if she wasn't even herself.

Talking with customers and stocking shelves did nothing to alleviate her racing mind or inability to stop fidgeting.

"I'm going to get something from the bakery," she

said as she grabbed her wallet from beneath the front counter. "Want anything?"

Devon looked up from where she was emailing out the latest shop newsletter. "I wouldn't say no to a bear claw."

Thankful to get away from Devon's knowing glances for a few minutes, she strolled down the street then crossed over at the corner. When she stepped into the bakery and inhaled the heavenly scents of chocolate, cinnamon and vanilla, she felt herself relax and her mouth water. This was what she needed. If there was one thing that stood a chance of shoving the memory of being pressed close to Ben's chest from her mind, it was an infusion of sugar and carbohydrates.

Keri Teague, the owner of the bakery and wife of local sheriff Simon Teague, waved from where she was taking what looked like a tray of freshly baked turnovers out of the oven. "Be there in a sec."

Keri's sister-in-law, Josephina, was busy ringing up the order for a group of customers.

"What can I get ya?" Keri asked as she stepped up behind the glass-fronted display case.

"Were those turnovers you just pulled from the oven?"

"Yes, apple and cherry."

"Well, one of those apple pies has my name on it. And Devon wants a bear claw."

"Coming right up."

"Hey, Mandy."

She turned to see that one of the women who'd been paying for a purchase was none other than Shantele

Drayton Osborne. Just her luck. Next to Shantele stood her bestie, Fancy Drennan. Mandy still couldn't believe that anyone would name their child Fancy.

"Hi, Shantele. Fancy."

"Heard Ben Hartley ran into your car yesterday," Shantele said as she used her finger to scoop part of the icing off the edge of her pink-frosted cupcake.

"Yeah." Though she would remain civil, Mandy wasn't about to be her normal chatty self and invite more conversation with these two. Her dislike of them and how they'd walked all over people like her stretched back years, and they probably didn't even have a clue. Mandy had the ungracious thought that they rarely had a clue.

Shantele had such a history of self-centeredness that she probably didn't even remember the dress incident.

Mandy watched as Shantele licked the dollop of icing from the end of her finger and hoped she got fat.

"I wouldn't mind if Ben Hartley ran into me," Shantele said.

Red-hot jealousy shot through Mandy's veins like a torpedo. She didn't have any right to feel that way, but that didn't seem to matter.

"I'd think your husband would have something to say about that." Mandy somehow kept her facial expression neutral when she really wanted to revel in her zinger.

Shantele glanced at Fancy with a knowing smile then said to Mandy in a conspiratorial, faux whisper, "What he doesn't know won't hurt him."

The very idea of Ben with Shantele, especially after his admission that he'd once had a thing for her, made

Mandy want to take Shantele's cupcake and shove it up her nose. That wasn't very kind or ladylike, but hey, you felt what you felt.

"It's a small town. He'd find out." She let her words lie between them, letting Shantele wonder if Mandy might be the one to tell him. "Can't imagine the *tantrum* he'd have."

Mandy detected the slight narrowing of Shantele's eyes before she pulled her fake smile from her repertoire and said, "Always good to see you, Mandy. We're off for a day of shopping in Austin." She said the last as she and Fancy exited the building.

"And no one cares," Mandy said under her breath, but Keri evidently heard her because she laughed.

"Sorry. Never have liked those two." With good reason, but she wasn't sharing that particular story again. She was still surprised she'd told Ben the dress story, but she couldn't stand the idea of him maybe still liking Shantele.

"And maybe they sparked a little jealousy."

"Of them? Ha! You couldn't pay me to trade lives with either one of them." She'd rather live in an abandoned railcar and have people actually like her.

"But what Shantele said about Ben seemed to hit a nerve."

"Like I said, she's got a husband. Granted, I wouldn't have picked him, but married is married."

Keri placed Mandy's purchases in one of the white bags that sported the Mehlerhaus Bakery name and logo. "I don't think that's the part that brought out the claws."

"Ben's a nice guy. The last thing he needs is to get tangled up with that." She gestured with her thumb back over her shoulder toward where Shantele had exited the building.

"So maybe you have someone else in mind for him?"

Mandy stood across from where Keri now stood behind the cash register and stared at her friend. "You, too? Seriously, did the city council put something in the water that compels normally sane people to turn into matchmakers?"

"Hey, we just figured out Verona was onto something all these years."

"Oh, just give me that bag," Mandy said as she handed Keri the money.

Keri smiled, confirming that Mandy wasn't very good at hiding the fact that she did, indeed, like Ben. But she had to nip that in the bud before word got back to him through the grapevine and things grew super-awkward between them.

"Snatch him up before someone else does," Keri said as Mandy walked toward the door.

"Be thankful I'm addicted to your pastries."

Keri's laughter followed Mandy as she stepped out of the air-conditioning into the blast furnace of another superheated day.

On her way back to work, she veered off into the small park tucked between two of the storefronts and sank onto one of the benches that faced a fountain in the middle. She pulled out her phone and texted Ben.

Don't need ride after work. Visiting my mom.

She hesitated before hitting Send, wondering if she was overreacting. What if Ben was interested in her, or could be with a little encouragement? Did it make sense to walk away from that? Growing up in a single-parent home, she'd always dreamed of growing up to have a big family of her own, complete with a husband and lots of kids. So far none of that had come to fruition, so why was she freaking out at the first inkling of a real attraction she'd had in a while?

She knew why. Because building up the idea of a relationship in your head only to have it dashed sucked. Maybe a little like having your homecoming dress snatched away by the class bitch. Unfortunately, she knew that from experience.

Chapter Five

Mandy took her time walking the mile to her mom's rental house after work. Devon had offered to drop her off, but Mandy had declined by saying she wanted the exercise. Considering Mandy had been on her feet all day and it was still in the sweltering nineties outside, Devon wasn't fooled. But she didn't challenge Mandy beyond giving her a knowing look.

The fact was Mandy wanted the time to herself to think. She didn't want Devon's pushing or questions or having to hide her sudden but true feelings around Ben. If he knew how much she'd been thinking about him since the previous day, he'd probably think she was bat crazy.

But what if he instead saw it as a compliment? Or, better yet, had been thinking about her, as well. She had a whole new understanding of what Devon had gone through when she'd been hiding her true feelings from Cole, afraid admitting them would ruin the budding friendship.

By the time she reached her mom's small house, she hadn't come to any definite conclusions and was dripping sweat. If Ben saw her now, she wouldn't have to wonder if he was attracted to her. One look would turn him off forever, and she wouldn't blame him.

Since she was already hot and sweaty, she headed to her mom's garden to do some weeding. After shifts at both of her jobs, her mom shouldn't have to come home to more work even if she enjoyed gardening and had the greenest thumb in Texas. Even in years of drought or blight when every other gardener struggled, her mom managed to coax tasty life out of her rows of vegetables, fruits and herbs, and multicolored beauty out of the flowers surrounding the bland tan house.

Mandy worked until she felt every bit as dirty as the soil in which the plants grew. Using her key, she let herself inside and, after gulping down a full glass of water, headed for the shower. Her mind refused to ignore thoughts of Ben for long. As she closed her eyes and stepped below the stream of water, her thoughts shot to the feel of his broad, firm chest pressed close. If it had felt that good with multiple layers of clothing between them, how awesome would skin on skin be?

She made a frustrated sound. Having those kinds of thoughts while in her mom's shower just seemed wrong. Now, her own shower…

She slammed off the water, wondering if she was just going to have to go for it with Ben in order for her imagination to let her be.

As she dried off and put on a T-shirt and shorts she'd left in her old room, she heard her mom moving around in the kitchen. Time to stop fixating on fantasies about Ben Hartley and all his enticing body parts and focus on the conversation she'd been mulling having with her mom.

By the time Mandy reached the kitchen, her mom had a grilled chicken salad and a glass of lemonade on the table for both of them with a plate of brownies in between.

"Okay, that was fast," Mandy said.

"I heard the shower come on right as I walked in the door. I already had the grilled chicken and the brownies made."

Her mom had been in the house when Mandy had been imagining Ben's naked body in the shower? Yikes. She hoped her mom couldn't read that truth on her face like she so often could.

"Sit, and let's eat," her mom said, gesturing toward Mandy's chair. Once they were sitting, she continued, "So I guess by the absence of your car in the driveway that Greg hasn't fixed it yet."

"Nope. Couple more days at least."

"Will Ben continue to be your driver?"

Mandy dropped the fork she'd just picked up into her bowl and looked across the table at her mom, then sighed. "Honestly, you spend half your day in Fredericksburg and you still heard something."

Her mom smiled mischievously. "Is there something to hear?"

"No." She knew the moment she said it, the single word had come out of her mouth too quickly. The hopeful look on her mom's face confirmed it.

"He's a handsome young man."

"Yes, and one who I'd probably said a grand total of a hundred words to prior to yesterday."

"How many you reckon you've said to him since then?"

"Mom."

"What?" Her mom's innocent tone was about as believable as cows suddenly taking wing like a covey of quail.

Mandy picked up her fork again and pointed it across the table. "Do not get your hopes up. Ben and I are just friends, at most."

"Many a great romance has started that way. Oh, say, your best friend's."

"I think the two of you are in cahoots." And she might as well throw Keri in for a plotting trio. Possibly Greg, too. The whole town had been infected.

"Not yet, but there is strength in numbers."

"Can't a girl eat her salad in peace?"

"Very well, but just in case it matters, I think he's a fine man from a good family. You could do way worse."

Like the man who'd abandoned her mom? The father who'd only stuck around until Mandy was one year old and then disappeared for parts unknown?

"Moving on to other topics… I've been doing some thinking lately, and I'd like for you to quit one of your jobs, preferably the one in Fredericksburg."

"You know how I feel about that."

"I know you're afraid of not being able to pay your bills, but you're a better money manager than anyone on Wall Street. I know you've socked away a good amount that you don't even touch."

"You never know when you might need it."

"True, but it's also important to enjoy life, too." When her mom started to object, Mandy held up her hand. "Hear me out first. I think you should make jams and cookies and whatever else strikes your fancy that we can sell in the shop. I know Devon won't mind, and you can keep one hundred percent of the profits."

"I doubt I can replace my pay at the restaurant by making snacks, especially with the bakery right across the street."

"There are at least a dozen things I know you can make that Keri doesn't have in the bakery."

Her mom took a bite of her salad instead of responding.

"You work too hard, Mom. I'm grown and able to fend for myself now, so you can afford to cut back. I want you to enjoy life and some free time."

"I don't know what to do with free time."

"That's why there are cool things like Pinterest."

Her mom still didn't respond immediately. Granted, she was chewing her food, but Mandy got the distinct impression her mom was trying to think of a reply that would end this particular thread of conversation.

"I'll make you a deal," her mom said. "If you think I can make a decent amount by putting some things in Devon's store, then I'll think about quitting the dishwashing job."

"Awesome!" The thrill of impending victory raced through Mandy. She honestly hadn't believed her mom would cave so easily.

"I'm not finished. I'll agree to make that life change

if you agree to be open to a relationship with Ben. If it doesn't materialize, fine, not meant to be. But don't actively prevent it unless you decide he's really not your cup of tea, not that you're just afraid of admitting your feelings."

Mandy considered her mom's offer then nodded. If it got her mom to slow down enough to enjoy life, to not feel as if she was hanging on by a thread as they had when Mandy was young, then letting down her guard around Ben was worth it. She knew her mom wanted her to be happy, but Mandy had always been puzzled by how her mom equated happiness with finding the right guy after the way she'd been abandoned by Mandy's father. When asked why she never got married or even dated after that, her mom always said she didn't need a man to be happy, that Mandy was all the happiness she needed.

"I know that look," her mom said. "You and I are different people. You can't let what happened to me make you hesitant to try to find love."

Love? Who said anything about love? Animal attraction didn't necessarily mean anything other than physical desire. The truth was she really didn't know Ben all that well.

But now that she'd agreed to her mom's terms, maybe she could at least satisfy that desire.

BEN DREW THE SWIRLING, floral pattern that he would use as a guide in hand tooling the leather saddle in progress. He'd had to try half a dozen times because he kept making mistakes. Damn if his mind didn't keep wandering to Mandy and how disappointed he'd been when she'd texted to say she didn't need a ride home. The news should have made him happy that he didn't have to make another drive into town, that he could use that time to catch up on his work. But instead, he'd evidently been transported back in time to when he was a hormone-flooded teenage boy. For the life of him, he couldn't rid his mind of the memory of her pressed close to his body and how he wouldn't mind it happening again.

The door to his shop opened and he looked up to see his mom step inside. In her hand was a plate of food.

"You didn't come in for dinner," she said. "Thought you might be hungry."

He glanced at the time, surprised to see how late it was. "Sorry. Trying to do some catching up."

She placed the plate on the opposite end of his workbench and came to look at the pattern he was working on. "I'm always so impressed with your talent."

A sense of pride filled him at his mom's praise. "Thanks. Just lucky, I guess."

"It's more than luck. You work hard, too hard sometimes."

"I enjoy it."

"I know you do, but you might enjoy other things, as well."

He suspected he knew where this conversation was going and that he wouldn't be able to stop it, so he decided to meet it head-on. He spun on his stool to face her.

"And I'd lay down money you have a suggestion."

"I noticed you didn't pick up Mandy from work today. I was hoping maybe you two might go out."

"She texted and said she was going to her mom's."

"Ah. Do you like her?"

"She's nice enough."

"That's it?"

Ben sighed. "Okay, fine, I'm attracted to her."

His mom's smile carried the same warmth he remembered seeing and not quite understanding when he'd first been placed with the Hartleys. Even though it had been foreign to him, it had made him feel happiness and hope. It still had that effect, and it was part of the reason he worked so hard. His adoptive parents were great people. They'd stuck with him, even when he hadn't made it easy, and made him more a part of their family than his birth parents ever had. He owed them for that and never wanted to do anything that would make them regret their decision.

"I think she's a lovely girl. Are you going to ask her out?"

"I don't know. Doesn't make a lot of sense."

"Why not?"

"I've never thought about her that way."

His mom placed her hand atop his. "People change their minds all the time."

"I feel as if maybe that pigeon gave me a concussion or something." Despite the fact he'd told Mandy otherwise.

His mom chuckled at that. "I think it has more to do with timing. Things happen when they're supposed to."

He wasn't sure about that, but he wouldn't argue the

point. Especially not when he couldn't tell her the real reason he didn't want to get seriously involved with anyone local. Having to see someone after breaking up wasn't high on his list of life goals. And if Mandy was like most women who eventually would want to get more serious, it would only be a matter of time before they broke up. He just couldn't tell his mom why and break her heart. He hoped Neil and Arden had some kids to soften the blow before he revealed he didn't ever intend to be a father. Thankfully he wasn't the only child his parents had adopted and thus he wouldn't be robbing them of the joy of being grandparents.

She patted his hand before heading toward the door. "Be sure to eat your food before it gets cold. And don't work too late. You need your beauty sleep."

He acted offended. "You saying your son is ugly?"

"Not at all. You're a handsome man, and if Mandy Richardson has eyes, she already knows that."

"You sure are persistent."

"I take that as a compliment," she said as she passed through the doorway out into the night.

He tossed down his pencil and picked up the plate and fork. Now with the food staring at him, he realized his stomach had been growling for a while. He took them outside and sat in the old metal chair. With the sun long gone and a slight breeze moving the air, it was more pleasant than it had been in days. He thought about how this time the night before, he and Mandy had been doing their best handiwork with pink streamers.

As he ate his dinner, he tried to pinpoint exactly what it was about Mandy that had suddenly demanded all his attention. Of course she was pretty with her shoulder-length brown hair, soft features and blue eyes that always seemed to be looking for something to laugh about. There was a carefree way about her, even after he'd crashed into her car. That quality appealed to him, even though he sometimes had a hard time allowing it to come to the fore in himself. He could have fun, but a part of him was always thinking about work, about making sure his family never wanted for anything, that their future was secure. He and Neil were a lot alike that way.

He took a bite of broccoli casserole and looked up at the sky, at the sliver of moon above the barn. He wondered if Mandy was back home, if she was safely inside her little box of a house. No matter how surprising it might be, something had clicked inside him the day before while spending time with her. It was enough to make him worry about taking his mom's advice. He'd had the thought earlier in the day that maybe he'd ask Mandy out, just a casual date, but a little voice of doubt kept him from calling to ask. He'd always felt safer going on the occasional date with someone he met at the music hall, someone in town for one of the rodeos, women he knew weren't looking for anything more than one night and done. They'd have fun, there would even be attraction, but he'd never been unable to stop thinking about any of them.

By the time he scraped up the last of his food, he still hadn't figured out what he was going to do about it.

MANDY LOOKED UP as the front door of A Good Yarn opened. She didn't know why her heart rate kicked up a notch. It wasn't as if Ben was going to stop by during the middle of the day. She'd spent the night with her mom and thus hadn't seen him that morning, but he'd texted to say he'd pick her up after work. While part of her still felt guilty about his driving all those extra miles and taking time away from his work, she admitted to herself that she was looking forward to seeing him again.

Instead of the object of her way-too-frequent fantasies, in came several of their friends who also had businesses in the downtown area.

"Hey," Devon said as she walked to the front of the shop from where she'd been stocking embroidery thread. "What's up?"

"We've come to see what you all think of an event we're tossing around for Labor Day weekend," Keri said.

"A street fair with all the downtown merchants plus booths from other area businesses, independent artisans and craftspeople, food trucks, whatever else we can think of," said India Parrish, owner of Yesterwear Boutique.

"I personally think there should be a dunking booth." Elissa Kayne, who owned the local nursery and garden center, looked as if she might have some dunkees in mind already.

Mandy immediately thought how satisfying it would be to sink Shantele and Fancy, but they'd never deign to do something like a dunking booth. Not when they probably spent an hour each morning just on their hair.

"Sounds like a good idea," Mandy said.

"I agree," Devon added.

"Well, now that we have that settled," Elissa said, "what's up with you and Ben Hartley?"

Mandy nearly banged her head against the counter. How had something that was basically nothing taken on such a life of its own?

"He hit my car and now feels guilty, so he's given me a couple of rides. Greg should have my car finished soon."

"Speaking of Greg, did you hear he's offering a reward for information about the identity of the people who wrapped his truck in pink streamers?" Keri asked.

"A reward?" Mandy barely kept the guilt out of her voice.

"Yeah. I heard he was going to press charges for vandalism."

"What? Since when is the equivalent of TPing vandalism?"

"I agree. It doesn't seem like Greg," said India.

"Unless it's his way to dish out a little payback," Devon said.

Mandy caught how Elissa and Keri were staring at her. Did they know? How could they possibly know? Devon wouldn't have told them.

"I wonder where someone got that many pink streamers." The look on Elissa's face made Mandy want to fidget. It was as if she knew exactly what had happened and who had perpetrated it but wanted to hear Mandy admit it.

"Well, whoever did it, I think it was hilarious," India said.

"And high time someone did something like that to Greg," Keri added.

"Listen to that—the sheriff's wife advocating vandalism," Elissa said.

"A harmless prank is not vandalism in my book. It wasn't as if they keyed his truck or slashed his tires."

Mandy had just thought how thankful she was the conversation had veered away from Ben when Elissa leaned her hip against the front counter and gave her a mischievous grin. "So you're not interested in Ben?"

Mandy sighed. "Why does everyone think accepting a ride with someone automatically means you're on the road to romance?"

"Rides," Elissa said.

"What?"

"Rides, plural."

"Yes, because my car is still not fixed and it's not as if I can hoof it to work and back every day. I'd die of heatstroke about the time I got to the Wildflower Inn."

The front door opened again, thankfully customers this time. Their friends left with a promise to get back to them about details on the street fair. By the looks on their faces, particularly Elissa's and Keri's, they wouldn't let the subject of Ben go either. It was enough to make Mandy second-guess her belief that Devon hadn't said anything.

When the customers left with their purchases, she confronted her oldest friend. "Did you say something about what I told you regarding Ben?" Devon's look of surprise was so genuine that Mandy immediately waved off her question. "Never mind."

"Why are you so sensitive about this?"

"Honestly, I don't really know."

"Maybe it's because you're resisting the idea when there's no real reason to."

Mandy let that thought percolate throughout the day and had half decided to ask Ben out on a date when she received a text from him that he couldn't pick her up. Her heart sank until she saw the reason, and then she felt guilty.

At clinic with Mom. Rolled her ankle. Taking X-rays to see if broken.

She typed back, Sorry to hear that. Hope she's okay. No worries. Will get another ride.

Except that her mom was in Fredericksburg, Devon had gone home an hour ago and she wasn't about to ask for a lift from anyone who'd been grilling her about Ben already. She glanced around the shop and figured it wouldn't hurt to spend a single night here. Maybe it was even a sign that her plan to ask out Ben hadn't been a good one and she'd been saved the mortal embarrassment of his declining.

Chapter Six

"You need anything else, Mom?" Ben asked as he adjusted the pillow under his mom's foot.

She looked tired and a little pale, but she still smiled as she patted him on the cheek. "I'm okay. It's not as if I broke anything. Few days and I'll be good as new." She glanced around at his brothers and sisters and dad, all ready to jump to her aid. "I'm just going to rest and watch some TV for a while."

As they dispersed, leaving only their dad and Angel near enough to help should the need arise, Ben was thankful he'd been walking toward his truck when he'd seen his mom's ankle roll, causing her to fall on her way back from the garden. He'd been the only one around to help her with everyone else away from the house for one reason or another.

He strolled into the kitchen and nabbed one of the double-chocolate cookies his mom had made before taking her tumble. They were so good he'd normally be able to clean the plate of them himself, but the thought that his mom could have been more seriously injured or that she might have had to sit on the ground waiting for help for hours had zapped much of his appetite.

Adam came in behind him and snatched a cookie for himself. "What a day."

"Yeah. You know she's not going to want to stay off that foot either."

"We can't let her outside by herself right now, though. There was another sighting of that mountain lion a couple of miles away, over by the Francis place."

That wasn't good news, for anyone. His thoughts shot to Mandy. He needed to make sure she'd gotten home safely and that she knew the cat was still in the area. When Adam headed for the barn to check on the horses, Ben pulled out his phone and dialed Mandy's number. It rang three times before she answered.

"Hey, how's your mom?"

"Not a break, thankfully, but a pretty bad sprain. She needs to be off her feet for a while, which is going to be difficult for her. She's not a woman to sit around doing nothing."

"Sounds like my mom. I'm trying to get her to cut back on work, but she's been hesitant. Old habits die hard, I guess. May be some hope on the horizon, though."

"Are you at her house again tonight?"

"No."

"You're home, then. I'm going to drive over and check out the surrounding area. The mountain lion was spotted again today."

"Uh, I'm not there."

Not home and not at her mom's. Was she at Devon's? That probably put a damper on Cole's night. Or…

"Oh. Sorry if I interrupted your evening."

"No, I'm just doing some catch-up paperwork."

Now he was even more confused. "Wait. You're still at work?"

"Yeah. It's nice and quiet when we're closed and I can work without distractions."

"You've been closed for hours. You're not planning on spending the night there, are you?"

"It's not a problem. And world's shortest commute in the morning."

"I'll be there in twenty minutes."

"Ben, there's no reason for you to come get me."

She wasn't spending the night in a store not set up for overnight guests. "I'll be there in twenty minutes." He hung up before she could protest again.

AFTER A FEW hours alone, Mandy had finally accepted that her intense attraction to Ben was a passing infatuation and shouldn't be acted upon. But now she had to face him again because of that dang chivalrous streak of his.

She finished the file she was working on and closed down the computer. Left with nothing to do but wait, she paced up and down the aisles. Why was she letting herself get so worked up? It felt totally ridiculous—but not as ridiculous as her yelp when Ben knocked on the front door of the shop.

With her heart knocking against the inside of her chest, she made her way toward the front, grabbed her purse then unlocked the door. She placed a hand on her hip and looked up at him.

"Anyone ever tell you that you're stubborn?"

"More times than I can remember. Including you, if I remember correctly."

"I would have been perfectly fine here. We have a couch in the back that's darn comfortable." A sudden image of dragging him to that couch made her drop her gaze and start fidgeting.

"Well, I'm here now. Come on so we can go get something to eat."

"You haven't eaten dinner?"

"Nope. We got Mom settled and much to her dismay turned over the kitchen to Sloane. I figure eating in town is in my own best interest."

She stepped out the door and locked it. "Does Sloane know you talk about her this way?"

"Believe me, she's getting off easy. You should hear how she talks about me."

"I wish I had a sibling to trade insults with."

"Want to borrow one of mine?"

She laughed at that as she walked toward his truck. "You don't fool me, Ben Hartley. It's obvious you and your siblings are thick as thieves."

He shrugged as he rounded the front of the truck. "I guess I'll keep them."

Mandy thought that she'd like to keep him. Somewhere private.

"So, where to?" he asked when he slipped into the driver's seat.

"Don't care. I'm up for anything." Well, couldn't that be taken the wrong way?

"Fajitas it is."

"You know we could walk there."

"True, but I'm not gonna. Way my luck is going, I'd twist *my* ankle on the way." He started the truck, circled the block and drove the short distance down the street and parked closer to La Cantina.

When he held the door of the restaurant for her, Mandy's heart irrationally skipped a beat. Guys held the door for her all the time—grandpas, little boys and even the occasional handsome cowboy with whom she crossed paths. But having Ben hold the door for her did funny, fizzy things to her middle.

As they waited in the foyer, she struggled to think of something to say. She almost asked how his mom was but remembered she already had. Still…

"How long is your mom going to have to stay off her feet?"

"Not sure, but it's a doozy of a sprain."

"Well, if I can help in any way, just let me know."

"Thanks, but we should be able to handle it."

After they were seated and chips and salsa had been delivered to their table, she received a text. A quick peek had her shaking her head.

"Well, that was fast," she said, half to herself.

"What?" Ben asked before popping a tortilla chip in his mouth.

She debated whether to tell him but decided she was tired of being anxious where he was concerned. She was going to be her normal, open self and just see what happened. She extended the phone so he could see Elissa's message.

Hear you're on a date with Ben. Told ya.

Ben snorted. "She's taking after her aunt. Would have never guessed she'd follow in Verona's matchmaking footsteps."

What did that reaction mean? Was he dismissing the idea of them dating as nothing more than the goal of busybody matchmakers? Okay, only friends it was. Good to know before she did or said something to make a complete idiot of herself.

After they ordered, she glanced around the restaurant and thought she caught a couple of too-interested looks before the people turned away. Though it likely had more to do with curiosity about why they were together, it reminded her of the other topic that had filled her with stress throughout the day.

"I heard a bit of surprising and potentially problematic news today," she said, keeping her voice quiet enough that only Ben could hear her.

"What's that?"

"Greg is offering a reward leading to information about who wrapped his truck in streamers so he can file charges of vandalism."

"How much? Maybe I'll turn you in."

"Ben!" Judging by how she attracted the attention of the people at the surrounding tables, she'd spoken much too loudly.

Ben, drat him, just laughed. "I'm kidding, and he has no intention of filing charges. Too many people know stuff about things he's done."

"You sure about that?"

"He's just doing it to try to flush out who it is because he has no idea. That must be eating him alive. Have to say that's more satisfying than knowing he had to rip all those streamers off his truck."

As they ate, they talked about the saddle he was working on, the upcoming street fair and how she was trying to get her mom to slow down and work less.

"She works two jobs?"

"Yeah. When I was growing up, she had three. She probably still would but the little grocery store where she worked closed down when I was about twelve or thirteen."

"And your dad didn't help?" His tone was hesitant, as if he wasn't sure he should be asking such a personal question.

"No. He took off when I was one. We haven't heard from him since. I have no idea where he is or if he's even still alive."

"Sorry. I shouldn't have asked."

"It's okay. It's not a sore subject. I don't even remember the man. I feel more sorry for my mom. I can't imagine what it was like to be abandoned with a baby."

"Seems she did a good job of raising you on her own."

"She did. I've got the best mom in the world."

"I'd argue that point, though I'm sure your mom is a fine woman."

Mandy scooped a chip into her guacamole. "Ditto."

As the meal progressed, she felt herself relaxing. Sure, she was still superattracted to Ben, but she would be fine just being friends. She didn't have to follow in

Devon's footsteps on the whole friends-to-more-than-friends path. She didn't feel right letting him pay for dinner, but no amount of arguing on her part swayed him. And the young waitress took his side.

It was difficult not to wonder about more, though, when it seemed everyone watched them with knowing grins as they walked out of the restaurant.

"It feel to you as if half the people in there already have us walking down the aisle?" he asked.

Though surprised not only by his perception but also his acknowledgment of it, she laughed. "I swear some were actually humming the wedding march."

"Not sure why people around here can't understand people can be friends or even date without wanting to get married."

And just like that, his words popped a hole in the happy balloon of her evening. So he was one of those guys who didn't want to get married. Also good to know, if disappointing. Not that they were anywhere near that point. Heck, they hadn't really even been on a date.

"Yeah," she muttered, not knowing what else to say. It didn't seem the right time to launch into how she actually did want to get married someday and have a lot of kids.

To avoid any awkward silences on the drive to her house, she launched into some funny stories from the knitting group that met at A Good Yarn. She loved those ladies, but their combined age was about equal to Methuselah's.

"Oh, this is the best one," she said. "Cora Steenburgen's husband had been talking about them getting a place on a beach somewhere, then started teasing her that it should be a nude beach. Well, she was having none of that—said that he had to at least cover up his 'nether regions.' And she knitted him an honest-to-goodness thong."

"Oh, eww! Now, why did you put that image in my head? I'm going to have to bleach my brain when I get home."

Mandy laughed so hard that she had to hold her ribs. "That deserves payback of some sort."

"Um, you ran into my car."

"After I was hit in the head with a pigeon."

"Still milking that for all it's worth, huh?"

"Hell, yeah," he said.

His answer made her start laughing all over again.

By the time he pulled into her driveway, she finally had her laughter under control and was again wondering if she might ask him out. He didn't have to be the marrying type in order for her to enjoy some casual dating, right? She'd been overthinking everything since her unexpected attraction had made its presence known. She just needed to chill and have some fun.

She didn't expect him to cut the engine and walk her to her door, and yet she experienced a pang of disappointment that he made no move to do so.

"Thanks again for dinner and for the ride home, neither of which was necessary."

He looked across the cab at her. "So you've said, and you're welcome."

Not wanting to rob him of any more of the time he

needed to work or spend with his family, she opened the door and hopped out. "Good night."

"Good night." For some reason he sounded distracted, and she figured he must be thinking about what he'd do when he arrived home.

She already had her front door open when Ben turned off the engine of his truck. Her pulse jumped as she looked back at him.

"Hey, Mandy—"

The greenish-gold glow of eyes from the edge of the darkness drew her attention, and in the next moment she saw the mountain lion edge into the light, its focus on Ben, who didn't see him.

"Ben, watch out!"

Ben turned, the cat moved closer and Mandy reached inside the house and grabbed Ben's rifle all within the space of one breath. She brought the rifle to her shoulder and for the first time in her life fired a weapon.

Chapter Seven

Ben jumped at the sound of the shot, but he wasn't the only one. The big cat jerked then sprinted away into the darkness. Without taking his eyes away from the spot where the mountain lion had disappeared, he started walking backward toward Mandy's tiny house.

"You okay?" he called out.

When she didn't answer, he spared a glance toward her to find Mandy standing there with a wide-eyed, stunned look on her face.

"Mandy?"

"I'm fine," she said, but her voice disagreed.

He closed the distance between them and took the rifle from her. Even without touching her, he could tell she was shaking. He gripped her shoulder and guided her inside, following close behind with a searching look out at the surrounding darkness. The cat was probably still running in the opposite direction, but he wasn't taking any chances.

He closed the door, propping the rifle in the corner next to it.

"I shot a gun," Mandy said, sounding as astonished as if she'd just completed a triathlon.

"Yep, but that cat's lucky you're a terrible shot," he said, trying to lighten the mood.

She shook her head. "I didn't aim at him. I was afraid I'd shoot you instead."

"That would really beat the pigeon to the head."

She looked up at him then pushed both hands against his chest. "It's not funny. I thought that lion was going to attack you."

He sobered at her obvious concern, how the encounter still shook her despite the moment of danger being over.

"Hey, it's okay." When she bit her lip, he pulled her close and wrapped his arms around her. That she sank against him and didn't make a funny remark told him just how scared she'd been. "We're both safe."

Mandy tried to shake her head, but it didn't really work with her cheek next to his chest. Despite how a part of him wanted to keep her right where she was, he didn't prevent her from stepping away and taking the few steps available toward the back of the small structure. When she turned to face him, she planted one hand on her hip and gestured toward the outdoors.

"This wouldn't have happened if you'd just listened to me and let me stay at the shop."

Irritation flamed up inside him, but before he said something he couldn't take back, he remembered that this was how Sloane handled things when she felt threatened or was scared. She lashed out. Maybe Mandy used the same coping mechanism.

He crossed his arms and just stared at her, unwilling to give her more fuel.

Unlike with Sloane, his lack of response seemed to douse her anger. With a wilting exhalation, she sank down onto the small couch. He dropped his arms and sat beside her.

"If this hadn't happened tonight, it might have been some other time when I wasn't here," he said. "I really don't like you being here alone with that lion lurking around."

"I can't uproot my entire life. Not having my car is bad enough."

He pulled out his phone and started a text.

"Who are you texting?"

"One of the wildlife officers I know. They need to take care of that cat."

She suddenly gripped his arm. "Don't let them kill it. He's only doing what's natural."

Ben knew the end result depended entirely on if the cat was found before someone was hurt or worse, but he nodded before sending the message. He continued to stare at his phone as he considered his next words.

"I think you should stay at our house until the lion is caught."

"I appreciate your concern, but I'll be fine. Believe me, I'm not stepping foot outside the door. And I might be sleeping with that rifle right by the bed, as uncomfortable as that makes me. That or a skillet. I doubt he'd enjoy a skillet to the head."

Ben shook his head slowly. "Now who's stubborn?"

"Birds of a feather, I guess."

Her fear of a few minutes before had faded, leaving behind the personality that she must have had all along but that for some reason he'd only just noticed in the past couple of days.

"Would you like to go out sometime?"

She turned her head to look at him in a way that made him think that perhaps she thought she'd misheard what he'd said.

"You heard me right. That's what I was going to ask you before I was interrupted by 'Mr. Kitty.'"

She smiled at his use of her too-sweet moniker for the mountain lion. Then she looked down at the floor for a moment before nodding.

"Okay."

"Well, don't sound so excited about it."

She pushed at his leg. "Don't push your luck. I might change my mind."

He kept his mouth shut.

MANDY STARED OUT her kitchen window, wondering where her feline visitor of the night before was. The cat's second appearance had scared her so much more than the first. The fear she'd felt when she'd seen the cat creeping toward Ben still made her sick to her stomach.

But she had to say the night had ended pretty darn well, though his asking her out created a different kind of fear. She couldn't remember ever being this excited and anxious at the same time. And she didn't like not knowing why things happened, and she really didn't know why it was Ben who got her all twisted up inside and why now. It wasn't as if he was one of the rodeo cowboys who came to town and turned her head, someone she'd never met before. Some of her friends had fallen for just those types of men.

But then her best friend had fallen for someone she'd known for years, albeit someone she'd once had a crush on. Mandy had never thought much about Ben other than the obvious realization that he wasn't ugly. Of course she'd never spent much time with him either. Would she have felt this way sooner if she had?

Honestly, the answers to those questions didn't matter. The fact was she had the hots for him now, and his asking her out gave her the opportunity to do something about it. He wasn't going to be her Mr. Forever, but she didn't mind him being Mr. Right Now. There were certainly worse ways she could spend her free time. She just needed to be sure that her mom didn't think they were serious.

She paced the length of her tiny house a couple of times, and for the first time she wished it was bigger. But only because she needed more pacing room. What was she going to do with an entire day off when she was hesitant to go outside and didn't have a car at the ready? She might not make it to her date with Ben, whenever that ended up materializing, because it was quite possible she was going to go crazy from being trapped in a twenty-by-twenty-six-foot box.

With nothing to do, she looked up the number to the wildlife management office and dialed for an update on the search for the mountain lion. When the man on the other end of the line answered, she identified herself and why she was calling.

"You've got perfect timing," he said. "I just got a call that they tranquilized the lion about ten minutes ago. They'll be relocating him to a more remote area."

"How far away?"

"Couple hundred miles."

Mandy exhaled in relief, then had a troubling thought. "Could there be more than the one of them?"

"Not likely. There's no evidence of more than the one male."

"Thanks. You have no idea how you've made my day."

He chuckled. "Here to serve, ma'am."

Mandy felt as if she'd been sprung from solitary confinement and immediately went to open the front door. It didn't matter if it did feel like an oven outside, she was going to breathe fresh air. She was well aware that many times she'd spent an entire day indoors reading or watching movies with no thought to craving the great outdoors. But she supposed it was the allure of the thing you couldn't have, like chocolate cake when you were trying to lose a few pounds.

Or Ben Hartley in her bed right now when he was probably out doing whatever ranchers did.

"Ha! Where did that come from?" But she knew. Her attraction to Ben had been building from the moment they'd faced each other in the Primrose Café parking lot. That attraction had led to a lot of fantasies.

Stop thinking about a naked Ben Hartley.

But the image refused to vacate her mind. Oh, well, she had nothing better to do, so she might as well go visit. Maybe she'd see if his mom needed any help.

She'd claim she was just being neighborly, when in reality it would be one part paying him back for dinner the night before and all the rides to and from work and one part the opportunity to ogle. She was young and in her prime, after all. A bit of ogling was perfectly natural, maybe even a health benefit.

Her mom had taught her to never arrive at someone's house empty-handed, so she whipped up a batch of homemade cheese straws because she needed something that was easy to carry. And if Ben happened to like them, so much the better. She wrapped the bag of cheese straws in an ice pack so they wouldn't be ruined by the time she reached the Hartley ranch. She tossed the bag and her purse into a small backpack and retrieved her bike from underneath its cover beside the house.

Cognizant that the country roads didn't have more than a few inches of gravel shoulder, she was careful to listen for vehicles and to get past blind curves or hills as quickly as she could. In a couple of spots, she got off the bike and walked beside the road. By the time she reached the Hartleys' driveway, she thought perhaps she was insane. Why had she thought that showing up hot and sweaty would make Ben go, "Oh, yeah, I'm so glad I asked her out."

Oh, well, she wasn't about to turn around and retrace her route now. Considering she'd not even had the foresight to bring a bottle of water with her, she'd probably die of dehydration on the way back. So she needed to deliver the cheese straws, availing herself of the Hartleys' air-conditioning and a glass of water for a few minutes, at the very least.

Her stomach grew nervous as she made her way up the drive toward the stone house and adjacent garage. She spotted the barn and a few other outbuildings and wondered which was Ben's leather shop. An image of him in there working on a saddle wearing nothing but a pair of snug jeans had her thinking she might just have to stick her head in Mrs. Hartley's freezer.

Since there were so many members of the Hartley family, she was surprised to not see anyone out and about on her approach. Not even a dog came out to greet her. She leaned her bike against a tree and made her way toward the front door, fanning her face in an effort to relieve some of the heat that seemed to throb in her cheeks. Just as she was about to knock, she wondered if that was a good idea. What if Mrs. Hartley was home alone and she wasn't supposed to be on her feet? Surely they wouldn't leave her without at least one person to help her.

The sound of quick footsteps inside led her to believe it wasn't Ben's mom hurrying to the door. It turned out to be his younger sister Angel.

"Mandy?" She looked past her to where the vehicles were parked. "How did you get here?"

"Would you believe I took temporary leave of my senses and rode my bike?"

"Yep, you're crazy. Get in here before you melt." Angel stood back and ushered Mandy inside. Mandy thought she'd been thankful for air-conditioning when she'd arrived home the evening Ben had crashed into her car. That was nothing compared to now. She was in danger of figuring out time travel just so she could go back in time to lay a big ol' smooch on Mr. Carrier's face for inventing AC.

Angel led her to the kitchen, where Mrs. Hartley was sitting at the table with her foot propped up on another chair, a fluffy towel below it and an ice pack on top.

"Honey, you're as red as a tomato."

"I might have forgotten sunscreen." She really hadn't thought this trip through beyond "Ben is sexy. Want to see Ben," had she?

When Mrs. Hartley made to stand, Angel pointed her finger at her mother. "Don't even think about it."

Mrs. Hartley made a sound of frustration deep in her throat. "They're treating me like an invalid."

"Your ankle is swollen and purple. Mine aren't."

Mrs. Hartley shook her head then patted the table in front of the chair across from her. "Have a seat before you fall over."

Mandy placed the backpack into another empty chair and pulled out the cheese straws. "Thought maybe you could use some snacks totally devoid of nutritional value."

Mrs. Hartley laughed at that. "I haven't had a cheese straw in forever. I'm going to have to hide these or they'll be gone in two minutes flat as soon as the rest of the gang arrives."

Angel set a glass of lemonade in front of Mandy, and she barely resisted pressing it to her cheeks and forehead. "Bless you."

"So what brings you over here?" Angel asked as she slipped into the chair at the end of the table between her mom and Mandy.

If she wasn't mistaken, there was a hint of a grin tugging at the edges of Angel's lips. Was Mandy that transparent or had Ben said something? If the latter, what had he said?

And what was she, fourteen years old? This was obviously payback for how she'd teased and prodded Devon to go for it with Cole.

"Ben said you'd gotten hurt," Mandy said, directing her answer at Mrs. Hartley rather than Angel. "I wanted to see if I could do anything to help. I know running a place like this must take all hands on deck."

"We do need some help with the bull castrations," Angel said.

Mandy couldn't see herself, but she was pretty sure her eyes widened like those of a cartoon character.

Angel's immediate laughter let Mandy know that not only was she being teased but that Ben wasn't the only one in the family with a sense of humor.

"You should have seen your face," Angel said.

"That's just mean," Mrs. Hartley said. "I swear I didn't raise them like that."

"Now, don't you sit there and act as if you've never stretched the truth," Angel said. "I distinctly remember a time when you told me that carrots were candy. That's why the Easter Bunny liked them."

Mrs. Hartley grinned. "Got you to eat your carrots, though, didn't it?"

"But I haven't eaten one since fourth grade."

"Oh, well, it was a good run."

Mrs. Hartley took a bite of one of the cheese straws. "Mmm, that's good."

"I can't make them too often. I inhale them. I'd end up looking like a giant cheese straw."

"Nonsense. You're a lovely girl. I told Ben the same thing."

Mandy nearly choked on her cheese straw.

Angel shook her head. "At least I was trying to be subtle about it."

Mandy looked at the youngest of the Hartley siblings. "Sorry to tell you, but you weren't very successful."

Mrs. Hartley reached across and table and patted Mandy's arm. "I like you."

The feeling was mutual.

"Since you're here," Angel said, "do you mind staying with Mom while I go get Julia from the school bus?"

"Not at all."

"Thanks."

Angel had barely made it off the porch when Mrs. Hartley asked, "Have you cooled off enough that we might venture out to my garden? The girls say they've been taking care of it, but I'll admit I'm particular about my garden."

"My mom is the same way."

Mrs. Hartley nodded. "I remember your mom winning quite a few blue ribbons at the fair with her vegetables. She's got a magic touch."

"She does indeed. I'm trying to get her to stop working her second job and instead make food products we could sell in the shop. So far, she's only agreed to think about it." With strings attached, but Mandy wasn't going to tell Ben's mom about that little detail.

"We old ladies are set in our ways."

"You're not old."

Mrs. Hartley pointed at her ankle. "I sure felt it when I pulled that klutz move."

"You're supposed to stay off it," Mandy said, finally responding to Mrs. Hartley's earlier question.

"I have crutches, and if I stay in this house a minute longer, I might go completely bananas. I wasn't made to sit still."

"I'm beginning to think you and my mom are sisters separated at birth." Mandy retrieved the crutches from where they were leaning against the kitchen counter and handed them to the other woman. She gave Ben's mom a helping hand in standing and getting to the back door.

As they approached the garden, Mandy retrieved a sturdy metal lawn chair, not one of the flimsy fold-up types, and placed it at the edge of the garden. When Mrs. Hartley sat down, Mandy grabbed a five-gallon bucket and turned it upside down for her to use as a footstool.

Mrs. Hartley started to give her direction, but she stopped midsentence when she noticed Mandy had already begun to weed around some of the tomato plants.

"Well, I see you have experience in your mother's garden."

"Some of my first memories are of sitting in the garden playing in the dirt as my mom weeded and watered and generally coaxed the most she could from every plant."

"Sounds as if she understands that a garden is just like a pet or a child. They all need time, attention and a lot of love."

They fell easily into a conversation about all things gardening, and Mandy found it just as easy to talk with Mrs. Hartley as her own mom. When that thought bumped up against the one about how much the women were alike and how they both had fantastic gardens, an idea formed that made so much sense she couldn't contain her excitement.

Mandy sat back on her heels and wiped the sweat from her forehead. "I may have just had the best idea in the history of ideas."

Mrs. Hartley smiled. "Well, this I've got to hear."

"I think with the combined expertise you and my mom have, you two should start a farmers' market in town. You could sell your extra crops, invite others to do the same, maybe hold it a certain day each week or month and during special events like the street fair over Labor Day weekend." She shared all the ideas that had been floating among the downtown merchants.

When Mandy realized she was yammering on and on, she stopped speaking abruptly. "Sorry, guess I got a little excited. This might be something I could talk my mom into, especially if I had someone else on my side."

Mrs. Hartley smiled. "You're right. It is a good idea. Why don't you bring over your mom soon and we'll discuss it?"

Mandy was so involved in her conversation with Mrs. Hartley that she didn't notice Ben at first. But when she detected movement out of the corner of her eye, she turned to see him walking toward them.

"Hey," she said, bordering on giddy at the sight of him. "How did you get here?"

"Rode my bike."

His expression tensed. "Are you crazy?"

She felt her smile slide right off her face as if the sun had melted it.

He pointed in the general direction of the road. "With a mountain lion running around—"

She held up her hand. "They captured him this morning and he's being relocated a long way from here."

That news surprised him, but the storm clouds in his eyes didn't lessen.

"It's still not safe to ride a bike on that road." He pulled out his phone. Was he calling to verify what she'd told him?

"You don't believe me?" She felt her own irritation start to boil, and it didn't help that the patch of shade she'd been in earlier had moved away from her, leaving her in the baking sunlight.

"I'm calling Greg. He's getting your car fixed today, or I'm taking it somewhere else."

Honestly, in that moment she didn't know whether to be thankful she might get her car back soon or ticked off at Ben's attitude. Maybe there was room for both. She'd gladly accept the former, but she'd let Ben know that she wasn't putting up with the latter, no matter how good-looking he was.

Chapter Eight

"Just make it happen," Ben said to Greg before ending the call. When he turned back to face Mandy and his mom, it was to find strikingly similar expressions on their faces, ones that didn't bode well for him.

"You know, I think I'll go inside," his mother said after glancing over at Mandy.

He moved to help his mom but she waved him off. "I'm perfectly capable of getting myself into the house."

The extra edge to her words gave him pause. He hadn't heard that tone in quite some time, and it told him that she was disappointed in him. Because he was concerned for Mandy's safety?

Despite his mom's assertion that she was fine on her own, he did open the back door for her and only closed it once he saw she'd settled herself in the living room chair and propped her injured ankle on the ottoman. When he turned around, however, Mandy had gone back to work in the garden and wasn't paying him any attention. He took a moment to inhale a deep breath, long enough to realize that maybe he'd come on a bit too strong. But he hadn't known the cat was no longer a threat, and he hadn't been exaggerating when he'd said the road wasn't safe for a bike.

He watched Mandy's movements, and while they didn't seem angry, gone was her bubbly warmth. With another breath, he walked toward the garden.

"I'm sorry if I sounded like an ass."

She looked up at him, squinting against the sun. "I'm not an idiot, you know."

"I know that. I just don't like the idea of you getting hurt."

"And I appreciate it. That's why I'm going to let you off the hook."

A smile tugged at his mouth, but he did his best not to let it show. He was getting off easy and didn't want to spoil it. Instead, he gestured toward the garden surrounding her.

"Anything I can do?"

"Yes, actually. How good are you at carpentry?"

She proceeded to tell him about the plan to set both of their moms to work starting a farmers' market in town, and how they could use some display tables, maybe a sign. He had to admit, he liked the idea. Every member of his family was always looking for new ways to bring in more revenue streams to keep the ranch running and able to be passed on to future generations. None of them wanted to risk this ranch, which had been in the family since Woodrow Wilson was president.

"Think your mom will go for it?" he asked.

"I'm going to do my best to convince her, and I've got your mom as an ally. Wouldn't mind another."

"You've got my support, but I don't know that I would be any help with your mom."

"You might be surprised."

What an odd response. Maybe she just meant the more advocates, the better.

Mandy pulled one last patch of weeds and dusted off her hands. When she moved to push herself to her feet, he extended his hand. She took it, and in a moment of pure selfishness, he tugged her upward with a stronger pull than necessary, causing her to stumble into him. Of course, he caught her, wrapping his arms around her waist. He let his smile form when he heard her quick intake of breath and saw the surprise in her eyes.

"So, about that date."

MANDY DID HER best not to look guilty as Devon dropped her off at Greg's garage the next afternoon. Word was he still didn't know who had streamered his truck, and Mandy wanted to keep it that way.

Greg was putting air in someone's tire when he spotted her. "Go on in the office. I'll be there in a minute."

She stepped inside the small office, which was as completely male as the man who ran the place. A small counter held a cash register and credit-card reader. The walls were filled with a large-print calendar with a picture of a hot rod that looked like something out of an old ZZ Top video, posters for the local rodeos and various high school sports teams, and an ad for motor oil. In fact, the office had a bit of a motor-oil smell to it. Opposite the counter was a wire rack filled with a variety of junk food for sale.

"Guess I better give your car back before Ben decides I need my face rearranged," Greg said as he came through the door that led into the repair bays.

"He would never do that," she said, though he had been mighty irritated the day before.

Greg laughed a little. "I'm not so sure about that. Seems he's become your knight in shining armor."

She ignored his innuendo. "He was only concerned that I was riding my bike out on the road since I didn't have my car."

"Sounded like more than a concerned neighbor to me."

She could argue with him, but then how would she explain it when she showed up with Ben at the community movie night in the park, which they'd settled on for their date? So instead of saying anything, she simply shrugged and pulled out her wallet.

"No need for that," Greg said. "Ben's insurance covered it."

She couldn't help the sigh of relief. She chose to live her life simply, not working day and night as her mother always had, but that meant watching how she spent her money. She hadn't been planning on a big car repair bill and was thankful she didn't have to fork over the funds. Even though it was the insurance that paid, for some reason she felt as if she should thank Ben. She shook her head the barest bit, mentally laughing at herself. She supposed she could thank him for paying his insurance premium.

"Guess you heard about what someone did to my truck," he said, startling her.

Hoping she didn't have guilt written all over her face, she glanced up at him. "Yeah, saw the picture. That must have taken a lot of work to get off."

"Yeah, and when I find out who did it, they're not going to be loving life very much."

Mandy managed to nod, as if she agreed with him, while trying to see if she saw any mischief in his eyes that would validate Ben's belief that Greg was just messing with them. She hoped Ben was right. The last thing she needed was to be charged with vandalism. That should do wonders for customer flow at the store, and she didn't want to taint the business Devon had worked so hard to build.

"Well, good luck with that," she said as she accepted her keys.

She thought she saw a flicker of surprise in his expression but wasn't sure. Not wanting to linger, she said goodbye and headed outside. When she sank into the driver's seat of her car, it was remarkable how good it felt to be in control of her own transportation again. And yet a part of her would miss having Ben act as her chauffeur. She had to say it hadn't been a bad way to start her days. Safely in the privacy of her car, she allowed herself to wonder what it would be like to wake up next to Ben after a night of making love. She had no doubt he'd be good in bed. How could someone look that good, have a smile that turned her heart into a gymnast and not be?

With a muttered "whew" and a shake of her head, she started the car and headed to work, where she could hopefully replace the images of sexy times with Ben with stocking shelves and helping customers find just the right shade of yarn.

"YOU DON'T CLEAN up half-bad," Sloane said when Ben walked into the living room.

"Wait, was that an actual compliment?"

"Don't push your luck, buddy."

Before she could stop him, he reached over and ruffled her blond hair, an action she had always hated. Of course, that was why he and Neil always did it. Adam seemed to have more sense than they did and kept his hands to himself.

Sloane batted his hand away. "I take it back. If Mandy is smart, she'll send you packing."

"Sloane, you know that's not true," their mom said from where she sat at the kitchen table peeling potatoes. "They're lucky to have each other."

"Mom, we don't 'have' each other," he said, not wanting her hopes and dreams to run away with her. "It's one date."

"Say whatever you like, but I see how you watch that girl."

"She's been here exactly twice." Once the day she rode her bike over and then the next when she'd brought her mom to talk to his about the farmers' market. Of course, in the nearly two days since that second visit, he'd been trying to ignore the way his heart had filled at the look on her face when her mom had agreed to go forward with the market and quit the job that required her to drive to Fredericksburg almost every day. It'd been both the best feeling in the world and the scariest.

"That's more than enough time to see you really like her."

"Of course I do. She's nice. Who wouldn't?"

"Don't waste your breath, Mom," Sloane said. "He's got a stubborn streak a mile wide once he makes up his mind about something."

"You're one to talk," he said.

"I wonder if Mandy is the same way," their mom said. "Because I saw how she looked at you, too."

And how was that? Was he making a mistake going out with her? It was obvious she was a romantic. She regularly kissed a concrete frog in case it might become a prince, after all.

He'd just have to be clear that while he liked her, perhaps too much, their dating wasn't going to lead to happily-ever-after unless she could agree that happily-ever-after included no rings, no honeymoons and definitely no kids. Somehow he didn't think she'd be able to agree to those terms, and that was okay. At least that was what he told himself. He did his best to ignore the snarly feeling he got when he thought about Mandy going out with someone else. That wasn't fair to her.

"As much as it pains me to say it, this time Sloane is right," he said. "Don't read too much into this. Focus your attention on Neil and Arden's providing grandbabies or on setting up Sloane with someone."

"Hey, leave me out of this!"

"Don't think I haven't tried," his mom said with a long-suffering sigh.

"I'm going to the barn," Sloane said as she jumped up from where she was reading a magazine.

"Chicken," he said as she headed for the door.

"Jerk."

He was still laughing as he drove away from the house on his way to pick up Mandy for their casual, no-strings-attached, definitely-not-leading-to-marriage date.

"WILL YOU STOP PACING?" Devon said. "You're going to wear a trough in my floor."

Mandy stopped at the front end of one of the yarn shop's aisles. "You know I pace when I'm nervous."

"Why are you nervous? I thought you said this was nothing more than a casual date."

She had said that. Part of her even meant it, or at least wanted to. But there was something at play here that she didn't understand. Her feelings for Ben had gone from the faucet turned off to full blast in a matter of days. She thought about him all the time.

"I don't know." She flung her hands back and forth. "I have all this excess energy that is making me fidgety."

Devon grinned. "I can think of something that might take the edge off."

Mandy stopped moving and stared at her friend.

"Don't give me that shocked look. And don't tell me you haven't thought about it."

She couldn't, not without lying. Of course she'd thought about it. Who could look at Ben for more than two seconds and not have those kinds of thoughts?

Devon's expression grew more serious. "Are you falling for him?"

"I don't know. Maybe."

"There are worse things."

"I'm not sure about that. I've never felt like this before a first date, and that's not good because you know what I want when I really fall for someone. I want marriage, a passel of kids. I got the distinct impression Ben wasn't a fan of marriage."

Devon laughed a little. "What guy is before he meets the right woman?"

"Ben met me when we were kids."

"Same time you met him, and look how your feelings have changed."

Mandy made a sound of frustration low in her throat. "Will you please stop making valid points? It's really annoying."

Devon just laughed again before glancing out the window.

"Don't look now but here comes your hot date." She glanced at Mandy. "Just go with the flow and see what happens."

Why did that sound so hard right now? It was normally her life philosophy. But going with the flow vacated the premises when Ben stepped into the shop looking like the cover model from some sexy cowboys calendar. She didn't know why the combination of jeans, boots, a checked button-down shirt and cowboy hat revved up a woman's hormones, but at the moment she didn't care. She was just thankful for the combination.

"You look nice," he said by way of greeting.

She dang near uttered "This old thing?" before she mentally slapped herself upside the head. She'd actually gone up the street to India's shop and bought a cute new frilly top with a pattern of little purple flowers and denim shorts with lace trim to wear tonight. She couldn't remember the last time she'd bought new clothes she didn't actually need.

"Thanks. You, too."

He glanced toward Devon. "Hey, Devon. You and Cole coming to the movie tonight?"

"We might if Cole gets back from Austin in time. He's delivering a sculpture to a customer there."

"Glad that's going well. I can't imagine being able to do what he does. I'm lucky if I can draw stick figures."

"He never imagined it as the path his life would take either, but it's working out." Devon shifted her attention back to Mandy, making the unspoken point that her words could apply to Mandy, as well.

"You ready?" Ben asked, drawing Mandy's gaze back to him. Man, she could stare at him for hours, not that it would be awkward or anything.

"Sure." And she preceded him out the front door of A Good Yarn.

Go with the flow. Go with the flow.

By the time they got to the park next to the lake, the grassy area in front of the projection screen was already filling up. It wouldn't be dark for a while, but a band she didn't recognize was providing musical entertainment. Kids of all ages were running around playing and eating scoops of ice cream from the Ice Cream Hut a little farther down the lakeside.

"Here okay?" Ben asked, indicating a spot near the back of the assembled crowd.

"Looks good."

She helped him spread a quilt on the ground, and then he placed the cooler he'd brought on the edge of the quilt.

"I wish you would have let me bring something," she said. "I am able to cook."

"I'm sure you are, but Mom insisted. In fact, she threatened to disown me if I didn't let her provide the food."

"She shouldn't have been on her feet."

"You tell her that. She won't listen to any of us, though Sloane and Angel kept her sitting and providing direction as much as they could."

"Well, thank her for me."

"I think you already did by bringing up that farmers' market idea. She and your mom have been texting back and forth like two teenage girls."

Mandy smiled. "That makes me happy. Mom has always worked so much that I feel she's missed out on just having girlfriends and doing fun stuff. Even though the farmers' market will be work, it's actually something she'll enjoy and will allow her to mix and mingle. Who knows? Maybe she'll meet a handsome guy in need of fresh tomatoes or zucchini."

"She never dated after your dad left?"

Mandy shook her head. "She always told me that she didn't need anyone to make her happy except me. While that's sweet and she's an awesome mom, I wish she'd found someone else. Not for me—I was totally fine without a dad because it was all I ever knew—but for her. I even delayed moving out on my own because I was afraid she'd be lonely."

"Is she?" he asked as he placed plastic-wrapped sandwiches out on the quilt.

"If she is, she'll never tell me."

"Maybe we should put Verona on the case."

Mandy smiled. "Not a half-bad idea."

They continued pulling food out of the cooler, pausing to return the greetings of friends and acquaintances, many of whom wore knowing smiles. She tried to ignore the feeling that she and Ben were the main attraction tonight and not the comedy due to be shown on the screen when night fell.

She retrieved a couple of sodas in glass bottles and a container of brownies from the cooler.

"Did your mom think she was feeding everyone attending the movie?"

"Remember what I said about her not wanting anyone to go hungry."

"If we're trapped in this park for a week, we're safe."

Ben laughed. "I'm telling her you said that."

"Fine by me. I'm a tell-it-like-it-is kind of person." Except where her growing feelings toward him were concerned. She realized in that moment that what she felt was much more than an attraction born of Ben's physical attributes. It was his kindness, the way he talked about his mom even though she wasn't his birth mother, how hard he worked, his sense of humor. She decided then and there that the single women of Blue

Falls were either stupid or blind. Surely someone had tried to change his mind about holy matrimony.

Why was she even thinking about this? It was only their first date.

"Guess you're glad to have your car back," he said before popping a cube of cantaloupe into his mouth.

"Yeah, though my chauffeur was a decent enough guy."

"That right?"

Feeling a little more daring, she said, "Kind of cute, too."

He leaned on his elbow, a satisfied grin on his face. "Didn't know that was necessary in a chauffeur."

She gave him a wicked smile. "Doesn't hurt."

"Maybe that's how I can help bring more revenue into the ranch, start the Cute Guy Cab Service."

"I'd think two jobs were enough."

"Says the woman who asked me to add carpentry to the mix."

"Hey, that's for our moms. And it's a onetime thing."

Ben laughed as he looked up at her, appearing more relaxed than she'd ever seen him.

As they ate, he told her about how he got into saddle making, beginning with a simple leatherworking project during shop class in high school.

"Then I saw how much people would pay for a well-crafted saddle and decided to start learning how to do it myself in my free time."

When the screen finally flickered to life, Mandy realized how much time had passed while they talked about his work, hers and how many people had signed up to take part in the street fair in the short time since it had been announced. That was the thing about Blue Falls. Locals hadn't met a community event they didn't love. The way the night was going so far, she had to give two thumbs up to the movie-in-the-park idea.

The movie was a funny one, and Mandy noticed that she and Ben tended to laugh at all the same parts, even when no one else did. When they got a couple of odd looks from those nearby, that just made them laugh more.

"If we're not careful, we're going to be kicked out of here," Ben said as he moved closer to her.

"You're a bad influence," she said.

Someone behind them shushed them, which made her giggle. She leaned into Ben's shoulder to try to stifle the sound, but his hand on her neck froze the giggles as if they were water bubbles at the North Pole. She eased away from his shoulder only to find herself looking into his eyes. There was a brightness there that drew her, but somehow the knowledge that they were in the middle of what seemed like half the population of Blue Falls intruded and made her break eye contact.

After that, they grew quiet. She became acutely aware of how close he sat to her, of his warmth and how it was distinct even from the warmth of the night. When they both reached for brownies at the same time, Ben instead wrapped her hand in his. She continued to stare at the screen, but she couldn't for the life of her tell anyone what was going on between the characters. Every single one of her brain cells was locked in on the feel of Ben's fingers entwined with hers.

Honestly, the only way she knew that the movie ended was when people around them started to stand. She glanced at the screen and saw the credits rolling. As she nervously glanced at Ben, she noticed Simon Teague walking toward them. Though he wasn't in uniform, the fact he wasn't smiling in the way he normally did sent a jolt of concern through her. Was something wrong with her mom? Someone in Ben's family?

"Ben, Mandy," Simon said as he stopped beside the quilt on which they sat.

"Simon," Ben said as he stood, then helped her to her feet. "How's it going?"

"Fair." He shifted his weight from one foot to the other, as if he had to do something unpleasant.

Mandy's heart flooded with adrenaline. "What's wrong?"

"We've found evidence that you two were involved in a vandalism incident."

Mandy shot a glance at Ben in time to see him laugh a little.

"We have fingerprint evidence, and Greg wants to press charges."

Ben stared at Simon, a look of disbelief on his face. "You've got to be kidding me."

Mandy began to freak out as she became acutely aware of the stares of people around them. How quickly she was going from respected member of the downtown business community to criminal. The delicious food Ben's mom had made churned in her stomach.

"The law's the law," Simon said.

"It was my idea," she said suddenly, unwilling to

have Ben punished because of her impulsiveness. "I did all the damage."

"Mandy—"

Whatever Ben had been about to say was interrupted by laughter. Everyone looked toward the source to find Greg leaning against a tree, looking as if he might pee himself from laughing.

Ben and Mandy looked at Simon at the same time, saw the conspiratorial grin spreading across his face.

"You're both jerks," Ben said, but there was a hint of reluctant appreciation for the effectiveness of the joke.

"Yeah, I can live with that," Greg said.

While the guys were laughing, Mandy felt as if she might collapse with relief.

Chapter Nine

Mandy's heart rate still hadn't returned to normal by the time they reached Ben's truck, though she'd admit that she wasn't sure how much was due to temporarily thinking she might be headed to jail and how much was a result of the way things seemed to be changing with Ben. Every time he'd touched her throughout the movie, it had sent a jolt all the way through her. A jolt of hyperawareness and longing.

"You okay?" he asked as he stepped up next to her on the passenger side of the truck.

"Not sure. It felt as if my stomach dropped to my feet back there."

"You know this calls for payback, right?"

She shook her head. "Oh no, I'm not escalating this. I don't want to worry that the next time I'm having a nice evening a cannonball is going to land in the middle of it."

Ben took a step closer to her. "You were having a nice time, huh?"

Her breath caught. "Uh, yeah. It was a good movie."

He lessened the distance between them by half, making him seem so much taller. "That's all?"

"The food was good, too." Why couldn't she just say she liked how she felt when he touched her?

Because for some reason, it scared her half to death.

"It was," he said, so close now she feared he'd hear her pulse racing. "Only one thing missing."

"Wha—"

Ben's hands rested on her shoulders a moment before he lowered his lips to hers. She'd swear on her life she heard the sizzle and pop of her nerves short-circuiting. There had been kisses in her past—at least she'd thought there had been. But they paled in comparison to the gentle but firm pressure of Ben's mouth against hers, the way the efforts of a preschool baseball player would when compared to those of a major leaguer.

Her hands went to his ribs and she so wanted to let them roam. As visions of unbuttoning his shirt to find what he hid beneath danced in her head, she somehow maintained a hold on just enough sanity to not act on that desire. After all, they were out where half the town could see them.

As if he'd had the same thought, Ben eased away from her, planting a quick kiss on her nose before breaking contact altogether.

Mandy bit her bottom lip to keep from whimpering. When Ben gave her a grin that said he knew exactly what he'd done to her, she narrowed her eyes.

"Don't get too full of yourself."

He just laughed as he opened the door for her. She

rolled her eyes but allowed him to hold her hand as she heaved herself up into the truck.

Even with all the cars leaving the park, it still took less than five minutes for them to reach A Good Yarn. When Ben pulled into a parking space right in front of the store, he wrapped her hand in his.

"I had a good time tonight, too," he said. "We should do it again."

The fizzy feeling came back. "I'd like that."

They didn't make any definite plans and Ben didn't kiss her again, but when she got in her own car a couple of minutes later, she still felt as giddy as a chocoholic in the middle of the Hershey factory.

DESPITE THE FACT that he'd meant it when he told Mandy he'd like to go out again, the second date still hadn't happened a week later. Unless you counted the quick lunch they'd grabbed at the Primrose in the middle of the week. They'd both been so busy with work—her at the yarn shop and helping their mothers prepare for the inaugural run of their farmers' market booth, him with repairs on the ranch and making progress on saddle orders. And building the display tables and signage for the farmers' market. He and Mandy managed to at least text each other every day, but they were both falling into bed at night wiped out.

He couldn't help but wonder what it would be like to fall into bed with her. If their brief kiss was any indication, he'd be willing to give up a good week of sleep to find out.

He shook his head as he parked along a side street

close to the farmers' market's assigned booth space. One date and one kiss and he was already feeling a little too involved for comfort. Probably the smartest thing to do would be to just let time pass without going on that second date, but he didn't want to. Still, he'd need to keep the relationship in check. More than likely sex wouldn't enter the picture. He liked it as much as any man, but it was a step he didn't take very often because he didn't want to deal with the question that always accompanied it—how had he gotten the scars on his arms, chest and back?

He cursed under his breath, not wanting to think about the answer to that question.

"You okay?"

Ben turned his head to see none other than the object of his unexpected desire.

"Yep, fine. You're just in time."

She didn't look as if she believed him, but he pretended he didn't notice. He couldn't tell her what he'd really been thinking about. The side of the street sure wasn't the place to have that kind of conversation.

Attempting to push the past out of his mind, he lowered the tailgate on his truck and handed her one of the shallow wooden display boxes for the fruits and vegetables.

"We'll take a few of these up to the booth area and I'll get the tent set up."

"It's already up. Found another good-looking cowboy to do it."

Ben turned to face her. "That right?"

"Yeah, my mom likes him, too. So does your mom."

This thing between him and Mandy was casual, short-term, right? So why was jealousy worming its way through him? And why did Mandy have to look so dang good in a pair of yellow shorts and a green top? He was beginning to think she could wear a rain slicker and rubber boots and still make him want to sweep her up into his arms and carry her to the nearest bed.

Mandy laughed, bringing him out of his own head.

"What's so funny?"

"If I didn't know better, I'd swear you were jealous." She turned to head up the street, wooden box in hand. "And the cowboy's taken already anyway."

When they rounded the corner, he saw Cole Davis laughing with his mom, who'd insisted on driving herself into town but now sat in a lawn chair while Mandy's mom and Devon organized bags of produce and boxes of jams and treats that Ms. Richardson was giving a trial run.

"There you two are," his mom said, as if he and Mandy had taken too long to reach the tent because they'd been sidetracked by a make-out session. There was an extra layer of mischievousness surrounding his mom today, and from the smile on Mandy's mom's face, she was in total agreement.

If things were different, having both of their moms approve would be a good thing. Now he just feared it was going to lead to disappointment for everyone. Maybe he should cut things off with Mandy while he was ahead.

But was he really ahead? How casual was it if he thought about her all the time?

Not wanting to think about the answer to that question too much, he ignored his mom's teasing and began setting up the displays. As he worked, he listened to how easily all the women got along, laughing and sharing ideas about how best to display their wares. Mandy had told him that she was close to her mom, but seeing it drove home that point. And it caused a pang in his middle he hadn't experienced in a long time—a desire to have that kind of close bond with the person who had borne him. Not that he wasn't close with his mom, but she hadn't become his mom the moment he was conceived. There was no blood tie, no bonding from before he was even born.

But the woman who had given birth to him had no right to be a parent. Same with his father. Ben was glad to be alive, but he'd lost count of how many times he'd wished he'd actually been born a Hartley.

"Ben, honey, can you put these peppers in the display in front of you?" his mom asked.

"Yeah. You sit back down. Going to be a long day, and I don't want your ankle swelling back up."

She patted his cheek. "It's lots better. You worry too much."

"Then don't make me."

"Fine, fine," she said with a chuckle, returning to her chair.

Mandy stepped up next to him to arrange what looked like a few jars of strawberry jam on the table next to the display box.

"You're good with your mom," she said.

He nodded at her mother. "So are you, with both of them."

"I really want this to go well for them."

"They have enough combined determination that I don't doubt they'll sell every last thing."

She smiled. It was a simple, quick smile, but something about it hit him right in the chest and he couldn't help but think he'd like to see that smile every day. But he knew that kind of thinking was dangerous.

"I hate to run, but Devon and I have to get things set up at the shop. The knitting group is going to come in to do demonstrations."

He chuckled. "Just don't let Cora Steenburgen have her husband model anything she's made."

Mandy laughed so suddenly that she snorted. "Thanks for putting that image in my head."

"Hey, payback. I've been trying to get rid of it since you told me about it."

He tried without much success to keep his eyes from straying to Mandy as she and Devon walked away down Main Street toward the yarn shop.

"It better not be my wife you're watching," Cole said as he stepped up next to Ben. Thankfully he kept his voice quiet enough that the chattering moms behind them didn't hear.

"Well, she is a pretty woman."

"As is Mandy."

Ben hesitated a breath before nodding once. "Yeah."

"You sound as if that's not a good thing."

"No, it's fine." He situated a pile of squash in a row above the peppers.

Cole made an amused sound. "Don't want to get serious but she's making it difficult not to think that way."

It wasn't a question, rather what sounded like the

voice of experience. That Cole was now a married man provided more evidence that Ben needed to tread carefully and not let Mandy's pretty smile or the sway of her hips as she walked down the street make him forget why he was a no-commitment kind of guy.

IN BETWEEN RINGING up customers, Mandy stared out the window of the shop on the off chance that she might see Ben wander by. With him and his siblings all taking turns helping out at the farmers' market, it was conceivable that he might come see her during a break. But as the hours passed, none of the many faces she saw filling Main Street belonged to the man she couldn't get out of her mind. How many times had she relived their kiss? She'd lost count before she'd even gone to sleep that night.

And as if he wasn't attractive enough, he'd made himself even more so by how much he so obviously cared about his mom. So he was a good-looking, hard-working cowboy who had a great sense of humor and loved his mama. How was she supposed to resist that?

"Why don't you knock off early and go hang out with your hunky cowboy?" Devon said as she stepped up to the customer side of the front counter.

"I'm fine."

"Yeah, right. If you continue to stare out that window, your gaze is going to burn a hole in the glass."

"Well, that's an exaggeration."

"Barely. Really, I'm good here. You've not had any time to be together all week."

"It's not as if we're a couple."

"From my vantage point, you're well on your way. You just need to indulge in some more kissing sessions."

Mandy rolled her eyes. "I shouldn't have told you about that."

"You know you can't keep something that big from me. Besides, I've been told about the hot parking-lot kiss by no less than a half dozen people."

"So glad to be the latest entertainment for the town."

"It was like the dessert after the meal of watching you two sweat it when Simon said you were going to be charged with vandalism. I'll forever be sorry I missed it."

"I'm surprised someone didn't take pictures like they did of Greg's truck covered in streamers."

"I'm surprised Greg didn't record it."

"Jeez, that's exactly what I need, to go viral."

Devon smiled. "Seriously, get out of here. If I get busy, I'm sure one of the gals here will help me," she said loudly enough that the women of the knitting group could hear.

The ladies all nodded.

"And while you're out there, see if there are any unattached hotties who might be interested in a more mature lady," Franny Stokes said.

"What happened to the guy you met online?"

"Turns out he was so boring I started to nod off during dinner."

"Bet no one would nod off during dinner with Ben Hartley," Cora Steenburgen said.

"Dinner?" said Opal Ritter. "Honey, I'd skip right past dinner with any of those hunky Hartley boys."

The older ladies all started laughing, and when Devon gave Mandy a raised-eyebrow, "Can you believe this rowdy bunch?" look, they started laughing, too.

Mandy nearly refused to leave again, but she stopped herself. The lure of spending more time with Ben won out, so she grabbed her purse and made for the door.

"Don't do anything I wouldn't do," Opal called out.

"Well, that leaves it wide open," Cora said.

The ladies fell into another round of giggles as the door closed behind Mandy.

Because there was such a good turnout for the street fair, it took longer than she'd planned to reach the farmers' market tent. But when she came within sight of it, her gaze went immediately to Ben. Her heart rate sped up, and there was no longer any doubt. Despite how whirlwind it all felt, she was falling for him. Was there any chance he might feel the same way?

She shook her head as she continued toward the tent, reminding herself that she needed to keep her emotions from running away. No good would come from letting herself feel too much when it might not be reciprocated, at least not to the same degree.

"Hey, you're back early," Ben said when he spotted her. His smile knocked a good-size dent in her determination not to get too attached.

"Yep, told Devon I was blowing the joint. I'd had enough."

"Young lady, you did no such thing," her mother said.

"Okay, fine, she told me to leave and enjoy myself. She and the knitters are holding down the fort."

"Did she now?" Mrs. Hartley said.

Well, it seemed the intervening hours hadn't lessened the moms' combined approval of the idea of her and Ben together. Maybe if she played dumb with them, she could convince herself she wasn't back here mainly because of one tall, dangerously handsome man.

"Yeah, there is some food on a stick calling my name. I had a bag of chips for lunch."

Mrs. Hartley nudged Ben. "Go get this girl some food."

"Yeah," Mandy's mom said. "We'll be fine here. We've sold a lot of what we brought anyway."

At a quick glance, Mandy noticed the stock was considerably less than when she'd headed to work. And it seemed the other few people who'd taken part in the farmers' market had done well, too.

"So it's been a success?"

Her mom met her gaze. "More than I ever imagined. You're going to get your wish."

Joy rushed through Mandy. "You're really going to quit the job in Fredericksburg?"

Her mom nodded. "As long as nothing drastic happens, I'm going to try things your way."

Mandy pulled her mom into a hug. "That makes me so happy."

Her mom patted her back before pulling away. "Now, you two go have some fun."

"You heard the woman," Ben said, making an after-you hand gesture. "I've seen half a dozen beef kebabs go by, and my stomach is rumbling."

"Well, I wouldn't want to stand between a man and his beef kebab."

They smelled the grilling meat and saw the smoke

rising a full block before they reached the land of juicy kebabs. Ben ended up getting two, and she selected one with shrimp instead of beef.

"Don't tell me you don't eat beef," Ben said.

"Beef is fine, but I have a deep and abiding love for shrimp."

As they made their way down the street, Ben told her how the farmers' market had enjoyed a brisk business all day, how their moms were already talking about when to have the next one and that several other locals had expressed interest in joining in the future.

"I'm so glad it's gone well. I knew it had to have done when Mom said she was going to quit her second job. You have no idea how relieved that makes me."

"I guessed by the big hug you gave her."

They stopped at the booth of a glassblower and Mandy's gaze went directly to a beautiful green hanging window ornament in the shape of a four-leaf clover.

"Oh, isn't this cute?" Shantele said as she swooped in and ran her manicured nails over the ornament.

"Yes, it'll look great in Mandy's window," Ben said as he reached past her and nabbed the clover off the hook where it was hanging and handed the artist enough money to pay for it. "Thanks for holding it for us."

Holding it for them? What was he…?

As if Shantele wasn't there at all, Ben handed Mandy the clover and steered her away from the booth.

Tears threatened but she hurriedly blinked them away. "Thank you."

"For what?" But he had a wicked grin tugging at his

lips, lips that she suddenly wanted to kiss in the middle of this crowd.

"You sure you have room for that in your tiny house?" he asked as he pointed toward the sun-catcher in her hands.

Mandy gave him a look of faux exasperation. "It's not *that* tiny."

Between the booths selling lemonade and hot pretzels, the size of the crowd increased, forcing Ben and Mandy to move closer together. When they bumped into each other, Ben's hand wrapped around hers as if they'd held hands dozens of times before. She didn't make eye contact with him, afraid she'd look like a lovesick puppy.

When they made it past the crush of people and entered the section devoted to carnival-type games, he didn't let go of her hand. She caught the occasional glance sent their way, but she didn't mind. It felt too good to maintain the simple contact that in some ways was more intimate than their kiss after the movie.

The sound of children laughing drew her attention to where several kids were throwing water balloons at each other. There evidently were no prizes involved. The kids just used tickets for the chance to throw water balloons and get each other soaking wet.

"You know, it's hot enough out here that I'm tempted to do that myself," she said.

Ben smiled at her, a devilish glint in his eyes. "I think once you're an adult, it becomes a wet T-shirt contest."

"On second thought…" She watched as one boy was

hit by a particularly well-aimed balloon in the middle of his forehead. He sputtered as water ran down his face. "Someday maybe I'll just have a bunch of kids having water-balloon fights in my front yard."

"That will make your mom happy."

"Over the moon."

"I'm just crossing my fingers Neil and Arden have some kids soon so Mom stops giving me that expectant look."

Something about how he said it gave Mandy pause. Should she ask the question that had immediately popped into her head?

"You don't want kids?" She supposed it shouldn't come as a surprise considering his attitude toward marriage.

He shook his head. "Nope."

He gave no explanation, and Mandy couldn't help the break that formed in her heart. Here was a reason—a big one—why she couldn't get attached to Ben any more than she already had.

Mandy hadn't truly realized how much she had allowed herself to fall for Ben until his words gave a virtual punch to all her hopes and dreams. She knew that was giving their short-lived relationship too much weight, but she couldn't help how she felt.

"Why don't you like kids?"

"I like them fine as long as they're not mine."

She thought she detected an edge of bitterness underneath his matter-of-fact response. What was that about? But something inside her told her not to ask. Someone would have to be much closer to him than she was—and was ever likely to be—to get that answer.

It was okay, really it was. The verbal splash of water in the face served to remind her that Ben wasn't interested in a serious, long-term relationship. She'd gone into things with him knowing that, but how quickly she'd managed to forget.

"So, deep-fried Oreo?" he asked after he finished his kebabs, totally unaware how a few simple words from him had dampened her mood.

She pulled together a smile from some hidden reserve. "Sure. You only live once, right?"

And who knew how many more times she'd have a chance to walk hand in hand with this man who made her heart beat at such an accelerated rhythm?

Chapter Ten

Ben took a step back and eyed the finishing touches he'd put on the saddle. Not bad, if he did say so himself. With each one, he was getting a little bit better. If he continued that way, hopefully he could command higher prices at some point. He found he wanted to show Mandy the finished product.

In the week since the street fair, they'd seen each other every day. For a bit after his admission he didn't want kids, he'd thought that would be the end of their… whatever it was between them. He'd seen a change on Mandy's face at that revelation, or at least he thought he had. If there had been any disappointment there, she had covered it quickly and they'd had a good rest of the day. And there was no evidence what he'd said had bothered her during all the rest of the time they'd spent together over the course of the week, definitely not whenever they kissed. And damn, those kisses had gotten hotter and longer each time, their hands exploring more and more. The night before, as they'd said good-night outside La Cantina after having dinner, he'd wanted her like he hadn't wanted anyone in a very long time. If ever. The woman was like a drug that he'd walked past a million times but didn't know how addictive it'd be until he got a taste.

But it wasn't just physical. Damn if he didn't like everything about her. He felt as if he'd spent a lot of time missing out by not looking at Mandy in that way. He knew he was treading dangerously close to a line he'd told himself he'd never cross, but he couldn't stop thinking about her. It wouldn't be wise to fall for her, knowing that she wanted a family, but he worried he was already halfway there. Maybe even more than that. There had to be some point of no return he couldn't go past, but he hadn't a clue how to identify that point. Why couldn't two people just have fun together without things getting too complicated? Damn feelings.

The door to the shop opened and there stood the woman who'd just been occupying his thoughts. And to make his fantasies start running around in his head like a pack of wild dogs, she was wearing a pair of pink shorts that showed off her legs really well.

"Hey," she said, giving him one of her infectious smiles.

"Hey, yourself. Didn't know you were coming by."

"Neither did I, but Mom asked me to bring over some samples of new things she's trying for your mom's opinion. Personally, I think it was a thinly veiled attempt to make sure you and I crossed paths today."

He shook his head. "They're very determined, aren't they?"

"That's one word for it."

"Can't say I mind you being here, though."

"That right?"

"Yes, ma'am." He rounded the worktable and pulled her into his arms. "And I think maybe it was your idea to come over here because you missed me so much."

She gave a little snort. "Now you're sounding like Greg."

"Ouch."

"You deserve it for that comment."

"I think we should stop talking," he said before lowering his mouth to hers.

He wondered if she'd sampled some of her mom's cooking because she tasted sweet, fruity. He deepened the kiss and pressed her more firmly against him. She moaned and that simple sound lit a fire in him. His hands found their way to her waist, then underneath her shirt to her warm, soft skin. Damn, she felt good. He wanted to strip her naked and make love to her right there in the middle of his shop, and by the way she was responding to him with moans and her fingers digging into his back, she was evidently on the same page.

The mental image of her naked, sitting on the workbench in front of him, made him growl. It felt as if they were two wildfires meeting up and exploding into an inferno.

When Mandy suddenly pulled away, he damn near stumbled he was so surprised. One moment she was totally into the kissing, the hands roaming, and the next she was widening the space between them. When she glanced toward the door, it hit him that Mandy possessed more common sense than he did. Of course they couldn't do anything here where anyone could walk in without warning. Angel would rip him bald if Julia wandered out here as she did sometimes and found her uncle naked with a woman. And he wouldn't blame Angel.

Still, he couldn't just turn off his desire, not when touching Mandy had his entire body revved up like a hot rod's engine. But when he spotted the color in her cheeks and the way she wouldn't meet his eyes, he also wanted to smack himself. She deserved better than being taken in a dusty workshop. She was the kind of woman who deserved romance, but he wasn't the kind of guy who was into romancing. It led to the sort of commitment he wasn't willing to give.

"I'm sorry," he said.

Mandy waved off his apology. "No. It was… I didn't mind. It's just that—"

"Someone might walk in."

"Uh…yeah." She glanced toward the door again. "I better go."

"You don't have to." He didn't want her to, even though keeping his hands off her would no doubt prove a challenge within the small confines of his work area.

"Things to do. I'll see you later." She left before he could think of something else to say.

And still without looking at him.

MANDY SAT ON her front porch listening to the wind in the trees and the rumble of thunder in the distance. She'd come out here to try to calm down, to think of something other than how close she'd been to giving in to what she and Ben both obviously wanted. She'd experienced desire before, but never in her life had it felt so *carnal*, so bordering on conflagration.

Ben had thought she'd pulled away simply because she was afraid someone might catch them. That was only partly true, and she couldn't help the hurt that he didn't realize the main reason. She was falling in love with him, a man with whom she couldn't have the life she'd always envisioned. She'd say it was the worst decision of her life, but it hadn't been a decision at all. It was as if her heart and body had run off and left her brain in the dust.

Things would be so much easier if what she was feeling was desire alone. There was a cure for that. But when things like love got tangled up with that desire? Well, that made her life a lot more complicated. Should she ease away from spending any time with Ben so he'd move on? Would she break her own heart in the process? Probably. But ending things before they progressed any further might prevent that break from turning into a complete shattering.

She took a drink from her wineglass and glanced at the concrete frog.

"Why couldn't you have turned into a prince before I got myself into this mess?"

Damn frog didn't respond. He just sat there staring out toward the creek as usual.

She finished her wine at the moment she heard the rain moving her way. With a sigh, she realized no matter how long she sat out here, she wasn't going to discover a perfect answer to her predicament. And she'd just get wet. As she stood, however, her ears detected another sound, one not made by Mother Nature. The headlights piercing the darkness made her heart leap. She knew the sound of that engine. Despite the fact raindrops had begun to fall, she remained rooted to the spot as Ben parked and stepped out of his truck. As he stalked toward her without hesitation. When he got close enough, she saw the determination on his face. Before she could form a single word, he'd erased the distance between them and pulled her into his arms.

The moment his lips captured hers, she melted into him and knew she couldn't walk away from this man. At least not yet.

She moaned into his mouth, which had the effect of throwing gasoline on a fire. The world would be perfect if she could just get him naked and run her hands all over his heated flesh.

"I want you," Ben said against her wet lips.

"The feeling's mutual."

The rain began to come down harder, soaking through their clothes. Not that it would matter once they got inside. But as she reached for the doorknob, Ben instead pulled her shirt over her head and lowered his mouth to the top of her breasts.

"Oh," she breathed.

Ben chuckled as he backed her up against the front of her house.

"We're getting wet," she said in between kisses.

"Yep," he said, sounding totally unconcerned.

She had to admit having a wet Ben in her arms wasn't a bad thing. The feel of his damp shirt clinging to his back lit another fire within her and she let her hands roam up his spine to the back of his head. He'd left his hat somewhere, allowing her fingers to tunnel through his short, wet hair.

Only when the rain became a deluge did Ben open the door and steer her inside, not letting go of her and barely breaking the contact between their mouths. The rain thundered against the roof, but the sound still wasn't as loud as her pulse beating against her eardrums.

"I think…" Kiss. "We should…" Breath. "Get rid of…"

"I agree," Ben said, obviously not needing her to finish saying the wet clothes needed to go.

Her fingers went to the front of his shirt, thinking she'd make quick work of his buttons. But what should have been an easy task proved difficult. She fumbled with the buttons so much that Ben chuckled, right before he unfastened her bra with a single movement.

"Oh, hush," she said, "or I'll kick you out."

"No, you won't," he responded before letting her bra fall away from her breasts and taking one in his mouth.

She couldn't help the deep sound of pleasure that escaped her. Of course he was right. There was no way she was kicking him out now, not until what they'd started reached its conclusion.

Mandy dug her fingers into the back of Ben's scalp, pressing him harder against her. He licked and sucked and gave her breast so much attention that she was in danger of reaching climax before she even got totally out of her clothes.

"Take off those clothes before I take a pair of scissors to them," she said.

Ben laughed at that but took a couple of steps back. He held her gaze as he slowly unbuttoned his shirt. She'd never witnessed a striptease before, but his movements and the wicked grin tugging at his mouth made her understand the allure.

Well, two could play that game. She took a slow step to the side as she unbuttoned the top of her shorts. One more step toward the stairs leading to the loft that held her bed, and she kicked off one of her sandals. Her mouth watered as Ben released the final button on his shirt and let it fall open. Have mercy, she wanted to put her mouth on every inch of those pectorals, the six-pack below and the V above his hips.

Ben's knowing grin reminded her that she needed to return his volley, so she rid herself of her other sandal and began to slowly lower the zipper on her shorts as she eased up the stairs. The grin fell away from Ben's lips, replaced with a look of hunger that sent such a rush of feminine power through her that it made her a little dizzy.

The slow-motion play ended abruptly as Ben yanked down the zipper on his jeans, toed off his boots and shucked absolutely every stitch of his remaining clothing in a matter of moments. Her gaze took in the perfection before her, lit only by the dim light coming from the bathroom. But she didn't need full light to see just how ready his body was for what awaited them at the top of the stairs. She'd never wanted a man so much in her life.

And yet she seemingly forgot how to move her feet

as she watched Ben walk toward her. When he reached her, his hands went immediately to the top of her shorts and pulled them down, underwear and all. As if through a fog, she lifted her feet one by one, allowing him to pull her clothing free. Her entire body heated a few more degrees when he tossed the shorts and panties over his shoulder.

"I suggest we get ourselves to that bed, or we're going to find out if sex on these stairs is possible."

That a very real curiosity about exactly that planted itself at the front of her brain made her wonder who she'd turned into. She'd never been this...naughty? Adventurous? Uninhibited? She wasn't sure of the right word for the current situation.

The messages from her brain managed to reach her feet again as Ben began to climb the stairs. Mandy took the last few steps into the loft. Ben was only a step behind, so focused on her that he barely managed to duck in time to keep himself from banging his head on the low ceiling. In the next breath, his strong hands were on her, gripping her hips and pulling her flush with his toasty skin. Her hands ran up his chest, loving the feel of all that masculinity at her fingertips. What would he do if she licked her way up those delectable muscles? Before she could find out, he captured her mouth in another mind-blowing kiss that she felt all the way to the tips of her fingers and toes.

Ben's arms encircled her as he lowered them both to the mattress. Feeling the length of his long, powerful body stretched out beside her threatened to overload her senses, especially when he blazed a trail from her mouth to her neck, making his way down her body. She'd swear her entire being hummed in response.

She stopped his downward progress by capturing his face between her hands and pulling his mouth back to hers. Their tongues mated. There was no other way to describe it.

In the midst of the haze enveloping her, she became aware of Ben sheathing himself. Where he'd managed to hide a condom on his completely naked body, she hadn't a clue. And for a moment, she remembered why she'd told herself she couldn't get closer to him. But after feeling him pressed to her like they were, nothing save a tornado blowing her tiny house into the creek was going to make her stop what they'd started. She'd deal with the emotional consequences later. Right now, her body demanded satisfaction. And if she was being honest, her heart wanted it, too.

Ben eased himself atop her, and their gazes latched on to each other. "Don't let me hurt you."

If he only knew that it wasn't her body in jeopardy right now. To keep from allowing her feelings to show, she lifted her upper half from the mattress and trailed her tongue down his chest, smiling when his body went rigid as her tongue flicked his nipple.

With a growl she felt as well as heard, Ben spread her legs and positioned himself between them. His mouth plundered hers as he pushed inside her. Words ceased to exist in her world as her entire mind focused on the feel of Ben moving within her, on her own reciprocated movement, the burning and tingling sensations everywhere his hands touched her, the furious beating of her heart as their pace increased. She dug her fingers into his hips, which seemed to urge him to go deeper and faster. And she realized that was exactly what she wanted. Her breath came in gasps as she came completely undone. Her release seemed to fuel Ben as he chased his own. In the next moment, every muscle in his body went rigid as he hurtled over the edge.

Reality tried to intrude as Mandy's heartbeat began to slow. Her thoughts drifted toward what she'd been thinking before Ben showed up. But all her attention shot back to the present when he pulled her close, her head resting on his shoulder. As she placed her palm against his chest and felt the beating of his heart, she knew she couldn't give him up. At least not right now. This felt too good to walk away.

Was it possible they could have more than a hot physical relationship coupled with friendship? Would he ever change his mind about having kids? Could she? People did it all the time, right?

"You okay?" he asked. "You're quiet."

"Maybe I'm thinking about how awesome that was. Or what I'm going to wear tomorrow."

"It better be the first one."

"And if it's not?"

"Then I might have to try again—after I recover."

She smiled. "It was—awesome, that is."

"I aim to please."

"I'd say you did, but I'm afraid too much praise will go to your head."

He chuckled then planted a kiss on her forehead.

The tenderness of the gesture felt more intimate than their lovemaking.

Mandy let her fingers wander leisurely over his flesh, over the occasional imperfection that didn't seem imperfect at all. She supposed a man who worked on a ranch couldn't expect to make it through life without a wound now and then. But as her fingers glided over his flesh, something changed. Instead of being relaxed in the aftermath of sex, Ben's body had tensed. As she wondered why, her fingertips sent a message to her brain and she realized that several of the scars on his arms and stomach felt similar. Curiosity had her lifting her head from his shoulder and eyeing the circular spots as best she could in the semidarkness.

Ben tried to roll away from her and off the bed, but she flattened her hand gently on his chest.

"Don't. Please." She wasn't sure what had made her say that, but some instinct told her she should.

Ben stared up at the ceiling, as if he was looking far beyond the roof and the rain and even the present. Cold settled in her stomach and she wasn't sure why.

"What happened?"

He took so long to answer she began to think he wouldn't, that he might leave instead and not allow her to stop him this time. But then he let out a breath that felt as if it had been pent up his entire life.

"My birth parents liked to use me as an ashtray."

Mandy barely kept herself from gasping. But she suspected that would be the worst thing she could do, that it would send Ben down the steps so fast she wouldn't be able to catch him. That he would walk out of her life and not look back.

"Then I'm glad you're not with them."

Ben turned his head to look at her, confusion written all over his expression. "You don't seem surprised."

"Unfortunately, it's not surprising anymore when I hear about parents abusing their children. I don't understand it, never will, but it's in the news every day. Some people just shouldn't have kids, though I'm personally glad you're here. I wish you hadn't gone through what you did, but—"

He cut her off by rolling her onto her back and kissing her so thoroughly her head spun. When he finally allowed her to breathe, she stared up at him, in that moment loving him even more.

"What was that for?"

"You're amazing," he said.

"Thanks. Every girl likes to hear that." She ran her hand along his upper arm, feeling a couple of the cigarette burns and hating his birth parents with a ferocity she'd never felt before. "But there's nothing amazing about what I said. If anyone is amazing, it's you for living through it and turning out to be a pretty okay guy." She smiled, trying to lighten the moment even a fraction.

Thankfully, he smiled, too. And then he kissed her nose, her cheek, nibbled on her ear. She knew where this was going, and that he was probably using sex to purge his thoughts of what had happened to him. She tried to set aside wondering what kind of person could burn a child not only once but repeatedly. Was this the reason he didn't want kids? Could he possibly think he'd be the kind of person who'd injure a child? She couldn't imagine it, not in the least.

In a quick motion that seemed to surprise Ben, she pushed him onto his back. After holding his gaze for a moment, considering the wisdom of her next move, she lowered her lips to one of the scars and kissed it. Ben tensed, seemed to hold his breath for a long moment, but he didn't say anything or make a move to extricate himself. So she allowed her lips to travel to the next scar, then the next like the most horrible game of connect the dots ever. It took all her willpower not to cry at the evidence of what his parents had done to him. Thank God he'd gotten away from them and found a family who showed him the love he deserved. Who'd protected him instead of hurt him.

Ben remained still and silent as she trailed kisses down his ribs and up his arm. The location of the scars told her the beasts had made sure to put them where no one would see. She wasn't by nature a vindictive or violent person, but in that moment she had the thought that she'd like to show them what it felt like to have the burning end of a cigarette pressed against their skin.

Ben's hands threaded through her tousled hair and brought her mouth to his. They didn't speak, letting their bodies do the talking as they made love again, slowly this time. And she fell the rest of the way in love with Ben Hartley.

BEN LISTENED TO the rain on the tin roof a few feet above his head. With Mandy curled up next to him, her chest rising and falling as she slept, he thought that life in this little box of a house didn't seem so bad at the moment.

He still couldn't believe how she'd reacted to his scars, that he'd even told her the truth about them. He'd expected pity, and maybe she had felt some but she hadn't shown it. Instead, she'd kissed those constant reminders that he'd been a victim of the people who should have loved and protected him. She'd done her best to take away their power, to make him feel as if the scars didn't matter.

If he let himself, he could love her for that.

But the fact remained that they did matter because how they came about was the reason he couldn't give this wonderful woman in his arms what she really wanted. And he'd be a selfish bastard if he asked her to give that up for him. But damn if a part of him, a really big part if he was being honest, wanted to ask her exactly that. Because he couldn't remember ever feeling how he did right now—relaxed, happy to his core, at peace. He knew it would end as soon as they left this bed. He dreaded the daylight when he might see that pity in her eyes she'd been able to hide as they made love.

"Are you thinking about what a fabulous idea it was to come over here tonight?" she asked, her words still heavy with sleep.

"How did you know?"

"Because I was thinking the same thing."

He kissed her forehead as if he'd done it hundreds of times before, as if it was the most normal thing in the world. And he realized the fact that it came too easily was a problem. But how did he tell her that without it sounding as if he'd just used her for sex?

"Can I ask you something personal?" she asked.

"Okay." He didn't have to think too hard to guess what this was going to be about.

"What your birth parents did to you—you're not afraid you'll be the same way, are you?"

For a moment he was confused, then realized that based on what she knew her conclusion made sense.

"No. I just don't want their genes passed on. I might not do that to a kid, but I can't guarantee that trait won't surface somewhere down the line."

But as he said the words, he wondered why it felt as if he was lying. Was it possible that deep down he did worry he'd be like them? Even now, all these years later, he could still hear them tell him how worthless he was as they pressed yet another hot cigarette into his flesh. He jumped at the memory.

Mandy placed her hand on his chest. "That could happen in any family."

"But the chances are higher when you know it already exists in the DNA."

"You don't know that."

"I'm not willing to take the chance."

She jerked in his arms, obviously shocked by his words.

"You're a good man, Ben. I have no doubt you'd be a good father."

He wanted to tell her how much her compliment touched him, but he couldn't give her false hope if she thought she'd change his mind. How could he make her see that without hurting her? Would he hurt her anyway because he hadn't been able to keep his hands off her?

"Why do you want to have kids so much after you've seen how hard it was for your mom raising you alone?"

"I don't plan on raising my children alone."

And that, in a nutshell, was why he and Mandy could never be more than what they had shared tonight in her little house while the rain drummed on the roof. By the look in her eyes, she knew it, too.

Chapter Eleven

When Mandy said goodbye to Ben the morning after they'd made love, she fully expected that to be the end. She'd even had a good cry about it before setting her mind to getting over him and on with her life. Easier said than done. And when he hadn't called her anytime during the day and a half following his departure from her house, it had hurt but she'd managed with a little help from a dozen double-chocolate cookies from the bakery. She'd sworn that her self-pity party would end the moment she popped the last bite of cookie in her mouth.

But the instant they'd spotted each other across the room at the music hall, all the pep talks she'd given herself flew right out the window like Ben's pigeon had. First came a dance and Ben's hands resting at the small of her back, then the two of them sharing a plate of cheese fries in a corner, and finally more of those kisses that turned her brain into one enormous hormone.

That had been a week ago. They'd seen each other every day since. It seemed as if they were officially dating without making it official. Their conversations never ventured close to the seriousness of that rainy night in her loft, and she'd almost convinced herself that was okay.

Almost.

She wondered if he was ashamed of his scars, of what had been done to him, and that was why he acted as if that truth had never been revealed. Mandy wanted to say something, anything that would make them a nonissue, but it wasn't up to her to convince him. He had to convince himself, and she didn't know if that was possible.

"I'd say penny for your thoughts, but I'm pretty sure I know without having to pay for them."

Mandy spun on the stool behind the front counter of the shop and met Devon's gaze.

"Am I an idiot?"

"Wow, didn't see that coming." Devon leaned against the end of the counter. "What precipitated that question? I thought things were going well with Ben."

"They are."

Devon tilted her head slightly. "But you want more, and he doesn't."

Mandy nodded. "I'd come to terms with the fact that the night we spent together was it, that I needed to move on because we weren't right for each other. We each want something the other can't give."

"I don't think *can't* is the right word."

"Can't, won't, it doesn't really matter. He doesn't want children. You know how much I do. So knowing that, continuing things with him makes no sense."

"Love doesn't have to make sense. It's more powerful than sense."

Mandy was learning that firsthand.

"What do you want me to tell you?" Devon asked.

Mandy shook her head and looked out the window. "I don't know, maybe that I should end things with him."

"I can't do that."

She looked back at her best friend. "Why not?"

"Because from where I'm standing, you two are perfect for each other."

"Then you're not looking very closely."

"I can see things more clearly than you think."

Mandy was still confused by Devon's belief that Mandy could make things work with Ben when the end of the day rolled around and she headed to her mom's for dinner. Ben had asked her out for tonight, and part of her had been thankful she had a ready excuse to avoid him. Of course, she didn't really want to avoid him at all, and that was the problem.

It took her mom all of thirty seconds to figure out something was wrong.

"You've always been easy to read," her mom said.

"So it seems. I really need to rectify that character flaw."

"It's not a flaw, dear. It's a reflection of your openness and honesty." Her mom handed Mandy a glass of cold water. "This about Ben?"

Mandy walked across the small living room and sank onto the end of the couch. "I'm afraid I've made a horrible mistake."

Her mom's forehead wrinkled between her brows. "Has he hurt you in some way?"

Mandy shook her head. "No, nothing like that. It's just... What if I've just picked the wrong man?"

"You mean like I did?"

"No, of course not." Maybe, though she hadn't consciously thought of it that way.

"Ben is absolutely nothing like your father."

"But he doesn't want children."

"He might change his mind."

Her father hadn't.

"No, I don't think so." She couldn't tell her mom why. That was private, not something to be shared even with her mother.

Her mom sat beside her and took Mandy's hand between hers. "All I can tell you is to follow your heart. You have a good one, and I don't believe it will lead you astray."

Mandy wasn't so sure about that as she sat on her porch again a couple of hours later. Her heart had led her to a fork in the road that was going to damage her no matter which path she took. She'd either have to give up the dream of a family full of laughing, smiling children or the man with whom she'd fallen totally, irrevocably in love.

BEN DISMOUNTED OUTSIDE the barn, hot and thirsty after a couple of hours of riding to check on the herd and repairing a water pump that wasn't working properly. What he wanted more than anything right now was about half a gallon of cold water, a shower and to go pull Mandy into his arms. He'd had visions all day of spending the evening in her little loft.

His stomach growled, reminding him of how little he'd eaten since breakfast. Sounded as if he needed to go through with their planned dinner out at a new place in nearby Poppy before they got anywhere near her tiny house. Even though the past two days of not seeing her had seemed to stretch a lifetime.

"Ben?"

He looked up to see a woman maybe a few years younger than his mom. Beyond her he spotted a car that had both a number of years and no doubt miles on it. She didn't look as if she'd be in the market for a hand-tooled saddle, but looks could be deceiving.

"Yeah. Can I help you?"

It was the oddest thing, but he thought he saw a flash of pain in her eyes.

The truth hit him with such a gut punch that he literally took a couple of steps back, instinct pressing him to put distance between them. She was older now, of course. But some shred of childhood memory erased the age that time had added to her features. Staring back at him was the face of the woman who'd brought him into this world seemingly for the sole purpose of having an outlet for her anger.

She swiped at a tear, and turned all the years of banked anger and hatred within him into a raging inferno. He shook his head. "No, you don't get to shed tears."

"I'm sorry."

He didn't know if she meant for the tears, how she'd burned him repeatedly or how she'd damaged him so much inside that when he'd first arrived at the ranch, he'd acted out against his parents before they had a chance to hurt him. He didn't care why she was sorry, or even if it was the truth.

"You need to leave."

"I came to apologize."

"I'm not the least bit interested in anything you have to say. You gave up that right the moment you first pressed a cigarette into my skin."

"I know I was horrible."

"You got that right."

"I'm not asking for forgiveness."

"Good thing because you're not getting it." Why was she even here? Why now?

"I just need to say the words, to let you know that if I could go back and do things differently I would."

"Well, you can't. You've said what you came to say. Now leave and don't come back." Ben knew he'd raised his voice when he noticed his mom and Angel come out onto the porch. He leaned in toward the woman he'd never believed he'd see again and lowered his voice. "I don't want anything to do with you, and you better not come around my family ever again."

He would never threaten a woman with harm, but he made sure there was no mistaking how he felt. Not even the sheen of tears in this woman's eyes moved him. At least that was what he told himself. Why would her tears make any difference when his hadn't to her? Well, he wasn't a defenseless child now. He towered over her and she didn't know what kind of man he was, if he might be violent like his parents before him. Even with everything she'd done, the idea that she'd see him as a physical threat turned his stomach. He took two steps back and looked toward the pasture.

"Just leave."

Christine—that was her name, one he hadn't thought about in a long time before he'd shared his past with Mandy—turned without a word and walked back toward her car. He didn't move. Neither did Angel or his mom. But he knew the latter would approach him at any moment, so he walked as calmly as he could manage back toward his horse and swung up into the saddle. He didn't make eye contact with his family as he turned the horse around and headed back out into the wide-open pastureland.

When he reached a point where the house and barn were no longer visible, he reined to a stop and stared out across the rolling hills dotted with cattle. Anger still surged through him, making him want to scream at the top of his lungs, to lash out. He couldn't see Mandy while he felt like a powder keg with the fuse lit. She didn't deserve to be exposed to the rage his birth mother brought to the surface in him. He didn't want her to see or hear anything else to do with his past.

His heart sank at the next thought. Had Christine shown up now, of all times, as a wake-up call for him that he'd allowed himself to get too close to Mandy? Yes, they had fun. She was sweet and beautiful and made him laugh. She'd made him feel as if his scars didn't matter. But she wanted kids, and he didn't. There was no getting past that.

He hated the idea of Mandy having children with another man, but that was selfish and not fair to her.

He had no right to stand in the way of her dream just because they had fun together.

But it's more than that, isn't it?

He shook away the thought, unwilling to let it take root in his mind. It would make it harder to do the right thing, break things off with Mandy. He was a fool for allowing their relationship to progress as far as it had.

Still, knowing that he needed to make a clean break, when he pulled out his phone he didn't call her. Instead, he took the coward's way out and texted that something had come up and he couldn't make it to dinner. He stared at the message for a long time before he marshaled the courage to hit the send button. As soon as he did, the anger bubbled to the surface again. After all these years, his birth mother was still burning holes in his life. This time, he had a feeling the scars were going to hurt a lot worse.

MANDY SANK DOWN into one of the chairs at the front of A Good Yarn and reread the message from Ben. He didn't go into detail, but he'd canceled their date. Ranching was an unpredictable business, so no telling what had happened to change his plans. She hoped it wasn't something bad.

She let her head fall against the back of the chair and stared at the ceiling. Of all the days for this to happen, it had to be the one when she'd finally decided to tell Ben how she felt, that she wanted to be with him even if that meant not having children. The truth was she still hoped he'd change his mind about that, but only time would tell. She just knew that with every day that passed, she loved him more and couldn't imagine life without him. Though he'd not said those words either, she believed that he felt the same. Being a guy, maybe he didn't even know it yet.

Or was it all wishful thinking on her part?

No, he wouldn't have shared the truth of his past with her if he didn't feel something stronger than physical attraction. It was too traumatic an experience for him to reveal it to someone with whom he was just having a fling.

With no date to look forward to, she took her time closing up the shop for the day. Then she decided that a big slab of chocolate cake sounded like a perfectly reasonable option for dinner and headed across the street to the bakery.

Keri was refilling a tray of cupcakes with fluffy pastel icing in the display case when Mandy stepped into the building.

"Hey, how's it going?" Keri asked.

"Fine. I'm in need of some truly decadent chocolate cake."

"Wooing your man with sweets—I like it."

"It's for me. Something came up at the ranch and Ben had to cancel our date tonight."

"Then chocolate is a good backup plan."

"I thought so."

But as she sat at home later eating her cake, she realized it paled in comparison to being held in the circle of Ben's arms, of laughing together at silly things, of reaching heights of passion she hadn't even truly known existed. As she looked around the confines of her tiny house, it had never seemed so empty and lonely.

Still, she'd had plenty of interests before Ben came into her life, and she slipped into her pajamas and settled in to watch the kinds of romantic movies that Ben probably wouldn't be caught dead watching. She laughed at the image of him curled up in bed with her watching a parade of romances.

Her days of work, helping out her mom and spending time with Ben must be catching up with her, however, because a few minutes into the first movie she started feeling drowsy. She smiled, thinking that maybe it was good to have a night away from Ben so she could actually sleep. She turned off her TV and snuggled under her thin summer quilt. As she closed her eyes, she wondered if she'd dream of Ben.

It wasn't even daylight yet when Mandy woke with her stomach churning. Oh, cake for dinner hadn't been a good idea after all. But as her stomach rolled again, she realized this wasn't just an upset tummy. She tossed back the quilt and raced down the stairs to the bathroom, barely making it before she threw up.

Ugh, she hated throwing up, couldn't remember the last time it had happened. When she finally stopped heaving, she was so tired that she couldn't pull herself up off the floor. Had Keri somehow made a bad cake? Even as Mandy had the thought, it didn't make sense. Maybe she was dehydrated? Had picked up a bug from a customer? Good thing she hadn't gone out with Ben the night before.

Ben.

Her breath caught as she considered another possibility. But they always used protection, both of them. Still, as she managed to pick herself up, shower and get ready for work, the queasiness and the what-if question didn't leave her.

But there was no way she was buying a pregnancy test anywhere in Blue Falls. So she left earlier than normal and drove the ten miles to Poppy, where she and Ben had made plans to go the night before. The town wasn't as big as Blue Falls, but its row of antiques shops were popular with tourists and decorators.

She pulled into the parking lot of a small pharmacy and tried to look casual as she walked up and down the aisles, buying several things she didn't need to camouflage the fact she had a pregnancy test in her basket.

Even though she didn't know anyone in Poppy, she breathed a sigh of relief when she returned to the car and put the town in her rearview mirror. When she got to work, she parked in the alley behind the building and used the rear entrance. Though she knew it was paranoia setting up residence in her mind, she felt as if anyone who saw her would know what she was up to, could see straight through the shopping bag to what it contained.

Once she was inside with the door locked behind her, she simply stared at the doorway to the bathroom. Was she just coming down with something and totally overthinking the cause of her nausea? Maybe it was because kids had been on her mind lately. Honestly, what were the odds that two types of birth control failed at the same time? Astronomical, right?

Still, better to know for sure that all was well than continue to drive herself crazy with worry. Even knowing that, her hands shook as she went through the necessary motions to take the test. As she waited for the results, it felt as if time had slowed like it did in those scenes from *The Matrix*. Finally, after she had aged at least a year, she glanced at the plus sign staring up at her.

"No, that can't be right." And yet she knew deep in her being that it was, that she was pregnant with Ben's child.

A child he didn't want.

She had no idea how long she'd been sitting atop the closed toilet seat when she heard the front door open, Devon arriving for another day of selling yarn and cloth and soap and everything that meant absolutely nothing to Mandy at the moment. How many times had she looked at the test result, convinced that this time it would reveal something different?

Devon called her name a couple of times, but Mandy couldn't scrape together the ability to reply.

"Mandy?" Devon's voice held concern as she stopped outside the open bathroom door. Mandy hadn't even taken the time to close it. "Are you okay?"

Mandy felt as if she moved in slow motion as she looked up at her best friend then held out the test. "I'm going to have a baby."

Devon's face registered surprise, and Mandy almost

laughed. No one could be more surprised than she was at the turn of events. Except maybe Ben. What if he thought she'd gotten pregnant deliberately? But that didn't make sense, did it? Because he'd used protection, as well.

"I don't understand why this is happening," Mandy said.

Devon helped her out to the couch that sat along one wall of the storage room and gave her a cold bottle of water.

"What am I going to do?"

Devon sat beside her. "What do you mean?"

Mandy picked at the cuticle on her thumb. "Ben doesn't want kids."

"That was when they were in the abstract. Chances are he'll change his mind now that it's a reality."

Mandy shook her head. "I don't think so. And… I mean, it's not as if we're headed down the aisle or anything." Neither of them had even said they loved the other. What if Ben didn't care about her as much as she did him?

"People don't have to be married to have children, but you don't know what the future holds. It's still early in your relationship."

"Exactly. Not the best time to say, 'Surprise! We're going to have a baby!'"

Devon took Mandy's hand and squeezed it. "Listen, just take it a step at a time. Make a doctor's appointment to verify the test result and make sure all is okay. Then just talk to Ben. He's a good guy, from a good family. You two will figure this out."

Mandy wished she had a fraction of the confidence Devon had that everything was going to turn out fine. She just couldn't help the sense of foreboding that had formed a tight knot in her gut.

Chapter Twelve

Ben cursed so loudly that Maggie, who was taking a nap in the shade of the barn, jerked awake and jumped immediately to her feet. The shepherd looked at him as if she didn't know him and he posed a threat.

"You'd cuss, too, if you scraped half the hide off your finger," he said as he eyed the blood welling. His hand had slipped off the wrench he was using to work on the tractor they used to deliver hay to the fields in the winter.

Maggie cocked her head at him.

"Okay, so you don't have fingers and aren't going to be using tools anytime soon, but trust me. It hurts like a bitch."

Movement at the entrance to the barn drew his attention, and he immediately realized he'd just cursed in front of his mom. "Sorry. I didn't realize you were standing there."

"Honey, it's not the first time I've heard bad words, and I'm certain it won't be the last."

"Am I getting my mouth washed out with soap?"

"I think you're a bit too big for me to manage that

now, don't you?" She moved closer to where he stood. "But I would like to talk to you."

It didn't take a genius to figure out why. "I'm sorry if I've been surly lately."

"Honey, you haven't been surly. You've been miserable."

That wouldn't have been the word he used, but he realized that she was right. Life had been going pretty darn well until Christine had waltzed back in. Even though he hadn't seen or heard from her in the week since that day she'd turned up at the ranch, he couldn't rid himself of the lingering anger that she'd thought he'd want to see her or hear one word she had to say.

And, damn it, he missed Mandy. He felt lower than low with how he'd handled things so far, either avoiding her calls or making excuses about why he couldn't meet up. He wondered if she'd caught on yet that he was brushing her off. Probably, considering he hadn't heard from her since yesterday. He really owed her an in-person explanation, but would that make things easier or harder for her? For him, he knew the answer. If he saw her, he'd want to pull her close. But to truly protect her and the dream she'd had her entire life, he had to let her go.

"I know you're not going to like what I have to say," his mom said. "But I think you should make peace with your mother."

"You're my mother."

"You know what I mean."

"No, I don't. Because it sounds as if you want me to make nice with a woman who thought it was a great idea to burn me repeatedly. And I have the scars to prove it."

He couldn't believe what he was hearing.

"You were enjoying life, enjoying spending time with Mandy until your mother showed up."

"Don't call her that."

His mom hesitated a moment, giving him an assessing look, before she nodded. "Fine—Christine. You're allowing your past to dictate your future. You're angry at Christine and miserable without Mandy."

Nothing escaped his mom's notice.

"There's a way to fix both of those things."

"I fail to see how."

"You need to talk with Christine. Both of you need to get out everything you want to say so you can move on."

"How can you say that? You know what she did."

"I do, and the mother in me, who loves you, wants to smack her—not going to lie. But I see how what she did when you were a little boy still eats at you, how it's made you feel as if you can't get close to anyone even when you find someone who is perfect for you."

"You're reading more into things than are there. Mandy and I… It was just casual dating, no strings."

"Bull."

Ben looked at his mom in surprise, at the certainty and strength of her single-word response.

"You care about her a lot, maybe even love her," she said. "And there's no sense denying it because I've got two perfectly good eyes thanks to these bifocals."

"She deserves better than me."

His mom shook her head. "Son, I don't know where

you get these ideas. I couldn't imagine that girl finding a finer man."

She didn't understand. How could she?

"But you do need to deal with your past before you stop avoiding Mandy like you have been the past week. And yes, I've noticed. We all have. You've been as prickly as a field of cacti."

"There's nothing that woman can say that will change the past."

"No, but maybe just by telling her all the things you've held bottled up inside all these years, you can finally move forward and stop living your life with a level of detachment. It's not healthy, and you'll never truly be happy." She walked forward and took his injured hand in her own. "I'll stop talking now except to say you need to go clean this and put some antibiotic cream on it."

Despite the topic she'd come out here to broach, he smiled at the last thing she said. That was his mom, the fixer of scraped knees and fingers, the dispenser of no-nonsense advice.

Except the idea of seeking out Christine didn't make any sense to him, none at all. But neither did the fact that he couldn't go five minutes without thinking about Mandy. Damn it, not one thing in his life made sense anymore.

MANDY LET THE cool water of the creek run over her bare feet, wishing that the flow would carry away all the heartache that had built inside her over the course of the past week. Though she hadn't wanted to admit it at first, she could no longer deny that Ben wasn't just busy. He was actively avoiding her, evidently done with her and what they'd shared. The irony was that he didn't even know she was pregnant yet.

And she was done trying to reach him so she could tell him.

The sound of an approaching vehicle made her heart leap, tempting her to believe she was wrong, until she realized it didn't sound like a pickup. Instead, her mom's car rolled into view. Even so, Mandy couldn't work up the energy to move from her little spot in the shade.

"Well, that looks like a good idea," her mom said as she walked down the slight incline to the creek.

"Yeah, I think we should install a creek in the shop so we can soak our feet in between customers."

Her mom smiled at that as she slipped off her own shoes and sank down beside Mandy. "Hope you don't mind me coming by unannounced."

"When have I ever minded that?"

"Well, I didn't want to interrupt if you had company."

The way her mom said it, Mandy could tell her mom had heard something and was fishing for information. "I'm guessing by saying that you knew Ben wouldn't be here."

"I wondered. I had lunch with Diane today. She seems to be under the impression that you and Ben are no longer together."

"She's right."

"What happened?"

"I don't know. You'd have to ask him." She considered whether she should reveal the rest, but it wasn't as if she could hide the truth forever. "I need to tell you something."

"You know you can tell me anything."

Mandy stared at her feet with the water flowing over them. Would she have to do this in the months ahead to reduce swelling?

"I'm pregnant."

"Oh, honey, that's wonderful."

Mandy looked up at her mom's unexpected response.

"Don't look so surprised. You've always wanted children, and I'm thrilled at the idea of being a grandmother."

Mandy shook her head. "I didn't want to do it this way. I had it all figured out. I'd meet a great guy, fall in love, get married and have a wonderful family. You'd have so many grandchildren you'd have a hard time spoiling them all."

"Sweetheart, there is still time for all of that."

"You missed the part where there's a great guy in the picture."

"Ben's a great guy."

"And we're no longer together."

The expression on her mom's face changed, darkened. "He doesn't know about the baby, does he?"

"No, but it doesn't matter."

"Of course it matters. He's going to be a father."

"It didn't matter to Dad." Mandy felt awful as soon as she said it. She started to apologize, but her mom stopped her.

"You're right. Your dad was not cut out for fatherhood, but Ben is not your father."

Mandy turned toward her mom. "Even if Ben wanted to be a father, I wouldn't use this to trap him in a relationship he obviously doesn't want to be in."

"I think you should at least tell him, talk about it."

"I've tried, but I'm not going to beg for it. I'll be fine. You proved that single mothers can be awesome, that they don't need a man to be able to raise a child well." If she couldn't have the man she loved, then she would pour all the love she had to give into being a mother. It would be enough. It had to be.

Her mom looked as if she wanted to say more, but instead she gripped Mandy's hand and smiled.

"You will be a wonderful mother. And we'll make it work."

"No." She had to make sure her mother didn't use this pregnancy as an excuse to go back to working another job. "This is not your responsibility. It's mine, and mine alone."

"It is no such thing."

"Mom, I just got you to lighten your load. I don't want you to feel like this is another burden you have to bear."

"First of all, you were never a burden. You've been the joy of my life. And I would never assume you couldn't provide for your little one. But I fully intend to shower him or her with love, and if you deprive me of the occasional babysitting duty, I'll never forgive you. It's been a long time since I've been able to snuggle a baby and breathe in that sweet baby smell."

Mandy smiled. "I'm sure there were times I didn't smell so good."

"Well, that's true. I don't care how cute a baby is, poopy diapers never smell like roses."

That made Mandy laugh, something she hadn't been able to do in days.

"Things will work out like they're supposed to," her mom said.

Maybe that was true, but Mandy couldn't help wishing that Ben could have been a part of that picture of the future.

BEN WAS CONVINCED he was never going to get another decent night's sleep again, and that was entirely his fault. It sure felt as if he was being punished and he deserved it. He'd told his mom that Mandy deserved someone better than him, and he'd proved that by the way he'd ended things with her. He needed to make that right, but his mom might also be right that he first needed to face the thing he'd been running from his entire life.

He rubbed his burning eyes as he drove toward the far edge of Austin where he was supposed to meet Christine at a public park. He hadn't thought meeting in a restaurant a good idea because some of the things he had to say...well, no one else needed to hear them. And he flat-out refused to meet her at home when he found out she still lived in the same place where he'd lived as a child. There was only so far he was willing to go to face the past.

As he pulled into the parking area, he thought about turning around and leaving. He still wasn't convinced that this meeting was going to make any difference. It certainly wasn't going to change his bloodline or the scars on his body. But damn if his mom's words about confronting the past before he could move forward hadn't burrowed so far into his mind that they refused to let him rest. So he'd do this, and then he'd apologize properly to Mandy and wish her all the best. And then he would put one foot in front of the other as he walked away for good, trying not to think about how much he missed her. Why did doing the right thing have to hurt so damn much?

He spotted Christine's car several spaces away and forced himself to get out of the truck. He'd swear his scars burned as he walked along the sidewalk into the heart of the park. Damn if he didn't have to remind himself he was a grown man now. He didn't have to fear this woman. She could no longer harm him. Even so, when he caught sight of her, he stopped in his tracks and once again considered leaving.

No, he'd come this far. Whatever the result, he was going through with this. As he drew close, he noticed something he hadn't when she came to the ranch. He'd been too angry to notice. She was pale, thin, didn't look well at all. It was the look of someone who'd lived hard.

When she spotted him, she started to stand but some instinct made him motion that it wasn't necessary. Even so, he didn't sit beside her. He walked to the opposite side of the pathway and leaned back against a bicycle rack.

"Thank you for coming," she said. "I was surprised to hear from you."

"No more than I was that I called."

She looked down at her hands, and he noticed how wrinkled they were. The only memories he had of her were cruel ones, but in them she was so much younger.

"Now that you're here I don't know where to start," she said.

"How about why you burned a defenseless child."

Her body jerked as if she'd been the one made to feel the lit end of a cigarette.

"We were drunk or high, maybe both. It's not an excuse, just a fact. We had no business having a child, but we did."

She was right about that, but for some reason he didn't say that out loud.

"I know nothing I say will make things right. I don't deserve forgiveness. But I'm telling the truth when I say I'm sorry and wish I could go back and do things differently. If you continue to hate me, I understand and don't blame you. Believe me, I hate myself, too. Always will."

He thought he should find some satisfaction in her self-flagellation, but he didn't. He just found it sad, a waste of a life that could have been so different.

"Why are you the only one here trying to make amends? I didn't get these scars on my body just from you."

"Your father died five years ago."

He didn't love the man, had in fact spent most of his life actively hating him, and yet the news that he was dead made Ben feel…sick for some reason. Was it just because Ben could never confront him like he was Christine?

"I wasn't with him anymore. I had been working to

get clean and sober, and he wanted no part of it. And it killed him. He was drunk when he drove through a barricade and off the end of an overpass that was being built. He injured a construction worker in the process."

That sounded about right for the man Ben had done his best to forget.

He noticed how she would only glance up at him, unable or unwilling to maintain eye contact.

"Did you ever think about me?" Why in the hell had he asked that? It was as if the question had formed in some corner of his brain he didn't know existed.

"Truthfully, not for a long time. I was too messed up. But I overdosed and nearly died. I know you may not believe me and that's okay, but that changed me. I got help. It hasn't been easy. I'm still tempted sometimes. But I work hard every day to not backslide into that life. When I got clean, it was the first time my mind was clear enough to even remember you. I wondered where you were, if you were with a good family. I knew anywhere had to be better than where you'd started."

Ben stared at her for several long moments, trying to figure out how he felt about her answer. No one liked to think their own mother never thought about them, but at least she was honest. How did someone even get to the point in her life where she was so messed up that she forgot she had a kid somewhere in the world?

"I've had a good life, great parents," he said. "Finally had a little luck on my side."

She continued to stare at her hands. "That's good. I'm glad."

Part of him hated that he was giving her any sort of

peace of mind, but then something shifted inside him and he suspected his mom had been right about him needing to face his birth mother and what had happened to him. He hadn't truly realized it was a wound that had been festering his entire life, but all of a sudden it felt as if he'd finally applied some antibiotic and given it a chance to start healing. That a dark weight had begun to lift the smallest bit.

"Is there anything you want to say?" Christine asked.

He thought of all the anger-filled things he'd said in his mind over the years, but none of them came out. "Why find me now?"

She shrugged, but then she looked up at him fully for the first time. "I did wrong by you, so wrong that it makes me sick now. Even if it made no difference, I had to tell you I'm sorry. It's as simple as that."

He wanted to stay angry, to continue to feel that ball of hatred deep inside him, but it suddenly seemed too damned exhausting to maintain. For some reason, he thought of Mandy's attitude about her absent father. He knew the man's leaving had made life harder for her and her mother, but they had made do. And Mandy wasn't a prisoner of a lifetime of anger toward someone she didn't even remember.

"I don't know if I'll ever want to see you again," he said.

A sad smile of understanding accompanied her slight nod. "I know. I'm just glad to know you have a good life and are happy."

As he drove back toward Blue Falls, her words echoed in his head. And he realized she was wrong. He wasn't happy, at least not totally. Christine might have done him wrong, but that didn't excuse the way he'd treated Mandy.

He pulled over on the side of the road and dialed her number. When his call went to voice mail, he shouldn't have been surprised. If she'd dumped him without a word, he wouldn't be quick to answer her call either.

"Hey, Mandy. I'm sorry I haven't called you back. I'd like to talk. Let me know when it's convenient for you."

There was a part of him that wanted to say more, but that would only make things worse. So he ended the call but continued sitting on the side of the road for several minutes, hoping she'd call back. His phone stayed silent. He should have known better. He allowed his head to drop back against the seat's headrest.

What a day. What a hell of a day.

MANDY FINISHED THE transaction for a group of ladies from Boerne who were having a girls' day out and had purchased an array of soaps and candles. She maintained her smile until they exited the shop even though she hadn't felt much like smiling lately. It wasn't helped by the fact that Ben had called and left several messages, and it had been harder than it should be to not call him back. In fact, she'd bet money that it was him causing the ringing of her phone right now.

She'd come to the conclusion that maybe he'd been right in just making a clean break. How smart had it been to continue things when they both knew they had conflicting goals for the future?

"You still haven't talked to him?" Devon asked as

she deposited a basket of essential-oil lip balms next to the cash register.

Mandy shook her head.

"You can't avoid him forever. It's a small town. And you're going to start looking different soon."

"I'm aware," she snapped, then exhaled audibly as she sank onto the stool behind her. "I'm sorry."

"It's okay. I know your emotions are all over the place now."

Mandy glanced out the window at all the people going about their business, totally unaware they were walking past someone who felt as if her life had been turned upside down and inside out.

"I know you and Mom don't understand, but I have to make sure I'm prepared before I see him again."

"What are you afraid of?"

She shrugged. "That I'll fall apart when I need to be strong. That it will hit me so hard that I miss him that I'll burst out crying. That I'll tell him I love him even though I know it's not reciprocated."

"Are you sure about that?"

Mandy shifted her attention back to Devon. "If he loves me, he has a funny way of showing it."

"Guys are weird. They are about as good at showing their feelings as a cow would be at flying a kite."

Normally that image would draw a laugh from Mandy, but she didn't feel much like laughing lately.

Devon leaned her forearms against the counter. "I know it doesn't seem like it, but I have this feeling things will work out."

Mandy wished that were true. She did need to talk

to Ben. Even though he didn't want children, he at least deserved to know that he was going to be a father. She'd make it clear that her telling him wasn't any sort of play for them to get back together. She wasn't one who believed people should stay together simply because they had a child. More times than not it didn't end well for anyone, including the child.

After work, she stopped to pick up a few items on her way home. And though she wanted to keep her pregnancy under wraps for a while longer, until she got used to the idea of impending motherhood, she nevertheless found herself drawn to the baby section of the store. She browsed past the cribs, marveled at the wee socks and smiled at bibs that sported sayings like Mommy's Little Angel and The Ladies Love Me. When she reached the section filled with adorable baby clothes, she couldn't help but caress the supersoft cloth between her fingers. The mothering hormones must already be flooding her body because she had the strong urge to fill her cart with little onesies, pint-size pants and dresses so sweet they threatened to give her diabetes.

Without thinking, her hand went to her stomach. This was really happening. She was going to be a mom. And sometime between now and when she gave birth, she had to perfect the lie that she was totally okay with doing it alone. Maybe by then it would be true. But thankfully she had about eight months to find a way to fall out of love with Ben Hartley.

Chapter Thirteen

Ben grabbed the new set of windshield wiper blades and headed toward the front of the store. He kept his gaze down, not wanting to make eye contact with anyone he knew and have to stop to chat. He wasn't in the mood. He'd been delayed by traffic getting out of Austin, where he'd met with a state congressman who was interested in commissioning a saddle. Ben hadn't even been able to fully appreciate the big step for his business because he was too focused on getting back to Blue Falls before A Good Yarn closed. He had it in his head that if he confronted Mandy there, she'd have to talk to him, give him a chance to apologize. His inability to do so was beginning to eat him up inside.

But the snarled traffic crawling away from downtown Austin had made him late getting back to Blue Falls, and the shop was already closed. He could show up at her house, but there was no guarantee she'd allow him inside. He'd thought about going anyway, even if he ended up having to yell his apology through the walls.

Or maybe he needed to take her unwillingness to talk as a sign from the universe that he should leave things as they were. He'd apologize via a voice mail for how he acted and walk away for good.

As he glanced up, he spotted her. Looked as if he wouldn't have to park himself on her doorstep after all. He was about to take a step forward when he noticed the section of the store she was in. The baby section.

The way she was looking at a little pink dress covered in ruffles actually made his heart ache. She was going to be a great mother someday. Never in his life had he wished so much that he hadn't come from the background he did.

He watched as she put her palm against her stomach. Was she imagining having a daughter someday who could wear that little dress? He remembered how much love had been in Angel's eyes when she'd looked at newborn Julia and knew Mandy would be the same with her own child.

But then Mandy glanced down at her hand on her flat stomach and the world slowed to a complete stop all around Ben. Was she…?

The way she'd avoided his calls, how she'd refused to call him back made a horrible kind of perfect sense.

She looked up suddenly and spotted him. For a moment, she stood as frozen as he was. Her hand fell away from her stomach and she let go of the dress. He watched as she appeared to take a deep breath before turning and walking toward him.

When she stood close enough to speak, she glanced around as if to make sure no one was within earshot.

"You're pregnant?" Saying the words sent a cold chill through him.

She straightened and met his gaze. "Yes, I am."

"How?"

"I'm assuming the typical way. Just stick us in the really-small-percentage column." She shifted from one foot to the other and crossed her arms. "Listen, I know how you feel about kids, so you don't have to worry about this. I don't expect anything. I'm living proof that a child doesn't need both parents to grow up fine."

She wasn't saying anything that wasn't true, but damn it if he wasn't growing angry anyway.

"Were you ever going to tell me?"

"Eventually. Not as if I could hide it for long, right? But it was obvious we were done, so I had time. No need to rush."

He detected someone approaching with a rattling cart and stepped out of the aisle to let the older woman pass by. When he felt like he could manage speech again, the search for the right words came up empty.

"I don't know what to say."

She smiled, but it wasn't the kind of smile he was used to from her. "You don't have to say anything. We tried to prevent this, so I'm not blaming you."

"But—"

"Have you changed your mind about having children?"

He didn't immediately answer, still not sure how he felt about the meeting with Christine and the apology she'd offered him. Did it change anything really? She might be sorry now, but she'd still had the capacity to do harm to her own child. And from what she'd said, his birth father had never changed. Could he be okay with passing on not only the predisposition for cruelty but also for substance abuse?

Even though he hadn't answered her, Mandy nodded her head once.

"If you ever decide you want to be a part of your child's life, I won't stand in the way of that. But also don't feel as if you have to be involved out of some sense of responsibility. It isn't necessary." She offered what looked like a shaky smile. "Goodbye, Ben."

His mind screamed at him to say something, to stop her from leaving, but he couldn't seem to corral a coherent thought. So he stood there in the middle of the store feeling as if he'd fallen against an electric fence while wet and naked.

And like the lousiest excuse for a man to ever walk the earth.

MIRACLES REALLY DID exist because Mandy made it to her car without falling apart. She even made it all the way home before she couldn't hold the tears in any longer. No matter how much she told herself that she could do this alone, the fact remained that in her heart she didn't want to. She wanted to share this with Ben, wanted to share her life with him.

She wanted him to love her. To believe in himself enough that his doubts about being a father would go away.

It was sad that she wanted it all so much when it was obvious from his avoidance of her that he didn't feel the same way.

She was still sitting in her car with tears streaming

down her face when she heard another vehicle. Her heart leaped. Had Ben followed her? Did he change his mind?

But a look in the rearview mirror revealed Devon's car. She swiped at her tears, not that it mattered. There was no way she could hide the fact she'd been crying. Why was Devon here anyway?

Mandy got out of her car the same time Devon did hers. Her best friend since childhood took one look at her and pulled her into her arms.

"I heard you saw Ben."

"That was fast, even by Blue Falls standards," Mandy said as she stepped out of Devon's embrace. "I suppose everyone knows I'm pregnant now, too."

"I don't know."

"Yeah, you do." She turned and walked toward the house then sank down onto the edge of the porch and patted the concrete frog on the head.

Devon sat beside her. "What did Ben say?"

"Not much. Said he didn't know what to say."

"I suppose it was a shock, like it was for you."

"I know." She sighed. "I'm not even mad at him anymore. Just…"

"Sad and heartbroken."

Tears welled in Mandy's eyes again. "Yeah. This isn't how I imagined my life turning out. I always imagined falling in love would be a two-way street."

"Do you want me to talk to him?"

Mandy shook her head. "No. I told him he didn't have to feel responsible because it wasn't his fault. He took precautions, and he never lied to me about how he felt about having kids. So it's not fair to saddle him with this."

"Saddle him… Do you hear yourself? Neither of you asked for this, so to my way of thinking the only fair thing is for you two to share the responsibility of raising this child. Even if you aren't together."

"You don't understand."

"Then enlighten me."

Mandy thought about the burns on Ben's body, how those early years of his life had scarred more than his skin. Maybe having kids wasn't the only thing he was scared of, even if he didn't admit it. Even if he didn't realize it.

"I can't. You'll just have to trust me."

Devon shook her head and made a sound of frustration. "I just want to shake the two of you because it's so obvious you're perfect together. I've never seen you so happy in your life as you were with him."

Mandy shrugged. "I'll just have to find a way to be happy without him. I'm going to have a little one to help with that."

After Devon left, Mandy made herself a healthy salad for dinner and returned to the porch to eat it and enjoy the peace of this little slice of the world she called her own. She would raise her child here, and who knew? Maybe the prince inside the frog hadn't appeared because he was waiting for someone else. Maybe she'd have a little girl, and her daughter would be the Richardson woman who'd finally get her prince and a happily-ever-after.

BEN WAS AT the kitchen sink washing up after mowing the lawn when his mother came stomping into the room—at least the best she could on her healing ankle—and slammed down two bags of groceries on the counter.

"You okay?"

She didn't immediately respond, just continued staring at the bags. Oh, no. He got the same sense of foreboding he'd gotten as a child when she'd found out he'd done something wrong and tried to hide it. She hadn't flown off the handle, but her disappointment had hurt worse than any spanking or grounding ever could have. Not that she hadn't dished out punishment, as well, but the disappointment had always scared him. He'd feared each time would be the one when his parents said enough and sent him back to the hell he'd come from.

He watched, holding his breath, as his mom slowly turned toward him. "Please tell me that what I just heard is wrong. Tell me that Mandy is not pregnant with your child and that you didn't abandon her."

His mom might as well have slapped him across the face and followed it with a swift kick to his gut.

"I can't."

"Benjamin Joseph Hartley, what in the name of all that is holy has gotten into you? I know you're not that kind of man."

"It's complicated."

"Not from where I'm standing. Mandy is a wonderful woman."

"Yes, she is."

"Do you not love her?"

He opened his mouth to respond but didn't know what to say. Did he love Mandy? Was that why he felt so damned hollow inside? If this was what being in love made you feel like, why the hell would anyone want it?

His mom stared at him, waiting for an answer.

"I never intended to have children."

"Why not? You'll make a great father."

"How do you know that?"

She looked genuinely confused by his question. "Because I raised you."

"But it's not your blood that runs in my veins."

His mom took a step closer then stopped and gripped the edge of the countertop. "What did Christine say to you?" She sounded like a mama bear ready to defend her cub.

"It wasn't what she said. It's what she and my… father did to me."

His mom shook her head. "You can't think you'd ever do something like that. I know you, Ben. Even when you were hurting and lashing out, you did not have that kind of cruelty in you."

He turned and faced the window over the sink. "How can I in good conscience pass on those genetics?"

"You listen to me," she said as she gripped his upper arm. "There are countless people in this world who were born to all kinds of bad parents, and they didn't repeat their parents' mistakes. It's a choice, not genetics. I would stake my life on the fact that you would never do anything to hurt your child. And you can teach him or her to be a good person just like you and Mandy."

She must have finally said everything she needed to

because she proceeded to put away the groceries without another word. He stood watching her for a moment, wondering about the right thing to do. He'd thought one way for so long, could he truly change? Did he want to? If he tried, would his lifelong fears let him be?

He felt as if he had a million questions fighting for space in his head but no answers. Not knowing what to say, he simply left through the back door and headed toward the barn. There probably weren't any easy answers lurking out on the wide expanse of the ranch either, but at the moment it didn't matter. He needed a ride to try to quiet some of the noise in his head. Maybe then he could find the answer within himself.

MANDY STOOD IN the middle of her tiny house and tried to envision where she would put a crib, how she'd make space for storing all the things that a baby needed. She imagined sleepless nights, exhausted mornings, worries about every cough and sniffle, about whether each cry came because of a tummy ache or something more serious.

How was she ever going to manage it all alone when simply thinking about it threatened to overwhelm her? She had an entirely new level of admiration for her mother.

Her thoughts drifted to Ben when she looked up at the loft. She hadn't heard from him since she'd told him the truth about the baby, so she supposed she had her answer about whether he wanted to be part of his child's life. He'd never lied to her, but it still hurt. She wished it was as easy to fall out of love with him as it had been to fall in.

The sound of an approaching vehicle drew her to the window. But it wasn't any of the usual suspects.

Her stomach flipped when she recognized Diane Hartley's vehicle. She really liked Diane, but she had no idea if this was a friendly visit or not. Chances were very good that Diane already knew she was going to be a grandmother, but Mandy wondered how she felt about that.

She pressed her hand against her stomach and took a deep breath before meeting Ben's mother at the front door.

"Hello, Diane."

"Hello, dear. I hope you don't mind me stopping by without calling first."

"Not at all. Please come in."

Diane stepped inside and her eyes lit up. "This place is adorable."

Mandy smiled at the other woman's obvious enthusiasm. "Your son thinks it's not big enough for human habitation."

"I love my boy, but he doesn't always know what he's talking about." Diane turned to face Mandy. "Fair warning—I'm about to stick my nose where it doesn't belong."

"Okay." Mandy probably should stop this conversation, but honestly, she was curious what Diane had come to say. Maybe a small part of her even hoped whatever it was would give her hope that Ben might change his mind. She knew the chances of that were small, but it was just going to take her a while to get over that tiny flicker of hope.

Mandy motioned toward the couch.

"Yes, let's sit."

Mandy noticed Diane's quick glance toward Mandy's middle, confirming that she did indeed know about the baby. Once they were sitting beside each other on the small couch, Diane took a deep breath.

"Now that I'm here, I don't know how to start."

"This is about the fact that I'm pregnant and Ben and I are no longer together, am I right?"

"Yes."

"I know you may want us to get back together. So does my mom. But I'm not one of those people who believes that two people should stay together just because there's a child in the picture. I'm sorry if you disagree."

"I don't, actually."

That surprised Mandy, and it must have shown on her face.

"I'm happy you're going to have a baby, but that's not the reason I think you and Ben should be together."

Mandy turned toward Diane and took one of the other woman's hands between hers. "I'll make sure that you're able to spend time with your grandchild, and I told Ben that he could be part of the baby's life if he wanted to. I don't think he does, however. I know he has his reasons, and—"

"Mandy, listen to me. If there were no baby at all, I'd still believe the two of you belonged together. I've never seen Ben as happy as he was when he was with you."

Was everyone she knew getting together to coordinate talking points?

"I think you read too much into what you were seeing. Ben broke things off before he ever knew about the baby."

"Because his birth mother showed up on our doorstep."

Shock hit Mandy square in the chest, followed quickly by anger and the need to find the woman who'd hurt Ben so badly when he was a defenseless child. "What? Why?"

"Remorse, evidently. She came to apologize."

"Well, that's too little, too late."

Diane smiled. "See there, you're quick to his defense. That tells me you care about him."

"Of course I care. No child should have to go through what he did."

"No, they shouldn't."

"I hope he sent her packing."

"He did, but I convinced him he needed to talk to her."

Mandy slipped her hands away from Diane's and stood, paced the few steps to the window. "Why would you do that? He shouldn't have to ever see that woman again. I've never met her and I want to rip her hair out."

"Because he has let what was done to him prevent him from believing he can have a happy, full future with a family of his own." Diane stood and joined her by the window. "It was my hope that by finally facing his past, he'd realize a couple of things. One, that he's not like his birth parents, that there is no reason to believe he'd be continuing some tainted family line. And, second, that he'd realize it was safe to admit he loves you."

Hope soared within Mandy, but she quickly tamped it down. "He doesn't love me. I won't call it a fling, but what we shared was temporary, casual."

Diane shook her head. "I swear, you're both self-delusional."

"Excuse me?"

"Tell me the truth. Do you love Ben?"

Mandy knew she needed to deny it so Diane would stop trying to go down this dead-end path, but she couldn't force the lie. It was just too big. Instead, the truth tumbled out.

"I do."

"Then I ask you to just give Ben some time. He's more stubborn than the rest of my kids put together, and that's saying something considering Sloane is as stubborn as a herd of mules."

"I don't think he will change his mind, even if he cares for me."

"I refuse to believe that. I have faith that love—for you and that baby—is going to eventually be stronger than all the irrational fears he's worn like armor his entire life."

After Diane left, Mandy sat on her couch, staring out the window at the fading light. She wanted so much to believe that what Diane said about Ben's feelings was true, but she feared allowing herself that much hope. If it ended up either not being true or if Ben never admitted it, she didn't think her heart would ever mend from the pain of that loss. She had to protect herself, protect her baby. If that meant closing off the part of herself that wanted to believe she'd have a happily-ever-after, she'd do what she had to.

"HEY, BEN," HIS MOM said as she put away the last of the leftovers from dinner. "Can you run into town for me tomorrow and pick up some stuff I ordered from the hardware store?"

"Maybe Angel can pick it up for you. I'm behind on work." Perhaps because he wasn't sleeping worth a dime and couldn't concentrate when he did try to work on the saddle for the congressman.

"Angel has plans to go to San Antonio tomorrow."

"Maybe Arden can get it, then. She'll already be in town at the paper."

His mom sighed. "Fine. Neil, can you ask her for me?"

"Sure. She won't mind, unlike some people."

What the hell was that all about? He glanced at his older brother and saw a look pass between Neil and their mom. As he suspected, his mom had noticed he hadn't been to town in days. He was too afraid of seeing Mandy when he still hadn't figured out the right thing to do.

Needing some peace and quiet, he left the house and headed toward his leatherworking shop. But even the shop wasn't the refuge it once was since his thoughts plagued him everywhere he went.

He was just beginning to shave the edges of several pieces so he could attach them to the saddle tree when the door opened. He sighed inwardly, expecting to see his mother when he lifted his gaze. Instead, Neil stood there.

Ben nodded in the direction of the house. "What was that back there?"

"I'm just going to pull a big brother here and lay it all out. You're being an idiot."

"Wow, tell me how you really feel."

"Everyone knows Mandy is pregnant, just like we all know you're in love with her."

"You can't know that. I don't even know that."

"Yes, you do. You're just too blind to see it for some reason."

Ben tossed his skiving knife on the workbench. Obviously, he wasn't meant to get any work done tonight either. "What do you want from me?"

"I want you to stop standing in the way of your own happiness, damn it." Neil walked to the other side of the workbench and leaned his hands on it. "What is going on in that head of yours?"

"I'm afraid I'm defective, okay? Mandy deserves better."

"Defective?"

"You know what my parents did to me. What if that sort of thing is genetic? What if when the kid is crying or misbehaving, I snap and do something awful?"

"That's ridiculous. Did you ever want to hurt Julia when she was a baby?"

"No, but she's not mine."

"That doesn't matter. You would never hurt a child. It's just not in you. I don't buy into that crap about genetics making you a bad person. Decisions do that. You can make the decision to be a better parent than the ones who made you."

Ben ran his hand over his face as he paced across the cramped space. He had the thought that Mandy's little house was actually roomy compared to his shop. But soon there would be a baby in that small home, as well.

Could there possibly be room for one more person? Were his mom and brother right? Was he just using his old fears as an excuse because he was afraid of getting hurt every bit as much as he feared being the one to do the hurting?

"I've probably ruined things with Mandy. I walked away at the worst possible time." Walked away just like her father had. He was such a fool.

"Only one way to find out."

"I don't know."

"Do you love her?"

Ben fiddled with a scrap piece of leather as he pondered that question. But he knew the answer, didn't he? He'd known it for a long time even though he'd been afraid to admit it even to himself.

"Yes."

"Then I suggest you start by telling her that and go from there."

His brother made it sound so easy, but it might very well be the scariest thing Ben had ever done in his life.

Chapter Fourteen

"Sorry," Mandy said to Devon as she came back out into the busy storefront from the back. "Seems as if all I do now is go to the bathroom."

"It's okay." Devon motioned over her shoulder at the customers milling about the store, filling their baskets with yarn, knitting needles, soaps and handmade cloth napkins in patterns perfect for the upcoming holiday season. "They haven't turned into a stampeding horde yet."

Mandy chuckled a little at the image of stampeding knitters as she made her way back toward the front. It was a gorgeous fall day, the kind where the temperature was comfortable and the sky a stunning blue. The kind that evidently made people want to shop.

Devon handed over a skein of yarn she'd gotten from the storeroom to a customer who'd ordered the color special then wandered over to where Mandy was re-stocking the candle display. Mandy lifted a pumpkin-scented candle to her nose and sniffed it.

"I'm so glad pumpkin isn't one of the scents that

makes me nauseated now. That would have just been cruel."

"True. Hey, I got you something to celebrate the baby." Devon pulled an envelope out of her back pocket and extended it.

"Is this you trying to get out of throwing me a baby shower?"

Devon laughed. "Oh, no. I will be throwing the most awesome baby shower Blue Falls has ever seen, but this is a little different than burp cloths and impossibly adorable baby outfits."

Curious, Mandy took the envelope and ripped it open. Inside was a single sheet of paper. "This better not be a clue in a scavenger hunt. I don't think my feet or my brain is up for it. This baby is already siphoning my brain cells and I'm not even showing yet."

"No scavenger hunts, though that is a good idea for a town event."

Mandy opened the sheet of paper and scanned what was written on it. Her breath caught and she had to read it again more slowly. Even doing so she wasn't sure she'd read it right.

"This doesn't make sense," she said.

Devon propped one of her hands on her hip. "Why not?"

"You can't give me part of the shop."

"It's my shop. I can do what I want to."

"But—"

"But what? You've worked here ever since I started this place. You do every bit as much work as I do."

"I haven't put capital into it like you have. Plus, what about Cole?"

"I love him, but I don't see him running a yarn shop, do you?"

"That's not what I mean. This would be taking money away from you two and any kids you'll have."

"Cole is totally on board. In fact, he said he was surprised I hadn't done it sooner. I feel ashamed I didn't."

"There's no need to feel ashamed. It's your store."

"And now it's going to be partly yours, and you won't refuse me if you don't want to make me mad. I plan to spoil your little one like no child has ever been spoiled by an auntie, so I might as well start before she's born."

Mandy felt tears well. That seemed to be another side effect of pregnancy—her emotions bounced all over the place.

"I don't know what to say."

"Say you accept, then ring up these lovely ladies. They look as if they have serious knitting to do."

Mandy glanced toward the trio of women headed for the cash register then grabbed Devon in a big hug. "Thank you. You're the best friend ever."

"I know."

Mandy laughed at that, blinked away her tears and got back to work. After cashing out a string of customers, she turned at the sound of the door opening again. Only this time, it wasn't a regular customer or a tourist. It was Ben.

Her heart leaped at the sight of him. He looked so good it took every bit of willpower she had not to run to him. But sanity prevailed.

"Ben, what are you doing here?"

"I tried calling a couple of times but couldn't reach you."

She'd seen his name on caller ID both times, but thanks to those erratic emotions, she hadn't answered. She was afraid she'd start bawling like a baby when she needed to hold it together. To cover the truth, she motioned to the filled store.

"We've been crazy busy. People are getting the jump on holiday shopping." She paused to point out to a customer where the cross-stitch floss was located.

"Can you talk?" he asked.

"Not right now. Maybe later." Why was she brushing him off when she'd missed him so much?

Because she was scared to her marrow about why he was here. Was it to finally tell her in person that he didn't want to have anything to do with the baby?

She started to head toward another customer who appeared to be seeking and not finding something on the list in her hand.

"I love you, Mandy."

She stopped, and it seemed as if everyone else in the store did, as well. Slowly, she turned toward where he stood halfway between the front counter and the seating area on the opposite side of the space.

"What are you doing?" She glanced around at all the eyes on them and felt as if she might faint.

"My sisters tell me this is called a big gesture." Ben took a couple of slow steps toward her. "I'm sorry for so much. For walking away without a word. For letting my past control me. Allowing you to think that I didn't care about you or the baby."

"Do we have to do this here?" she asked under her breath, as if that might have a chance of not being heard by everyone in the store.

"Yes, because I want everyone to know what a jerk I've been and how I don't deserve you, but that I hope you'll forgive me anyway. I won't lie and say that the idea of being a father doesn't still scare me because it does. But I hope you'll give me a chance to try. I'm determined to do right by our baby, to be the kind of father my dad has been for me."

She knew he didn't mean his birth father but rather the man who had taken in five kids from different families who needed a home and who had loved them like his own, taught them to be the kind of good, hardworking, loyal people they were. How could she deny her child a chance to be a part of that? But what about her own heart? Did he mean the words he'd said to her?

"And I don't want to just be a father," Ben continued as he reached into his pocket and pulled something out. "What I want more than anything is for you to give me a chance to be a husband, too."

Mandy gasped and brought her hand to her mouth as Ben lowered himself to one knee and held up what looked like a ring through her sudden tears.

"Mandy Richardson, I hope you feel the same. If not, I've just made a complete fool of myself and I'll deserve that. But I've never meant anything more in my life than when I say I love you and want to spend my life with you. Will you please marry me?"

Was this really happening? Did she dare believe that

something she'd imagined so many times was actually coming true?

"Say yes," someone called out.

It was echoed by someone else, then another voice, and soon so many she couldn't distinguish them, though she was pretty sure she heard an enthusiastic agreement by Devon.

But Mandy just stared at Ben, searching his eyes for the truth. And she saw it, the most beautiful truth she'd ever seen.

She nodded slowly.

"That's a yes?" Ben asked, so much hope in his voice that her heart filled her entire chest.

"Yes, I'll marry you."

Cheers filled the store, clapping and shouts of happiness and more than a few sighs of appreciation at Ben's romantic proposal. But it was all eclipsed by the beauty of the smile on his face as he leaped to his feet and pulled her into his arms. The kiss that came next made her feel as if he'd rocketed them into space and she was floating weightless. She kissed him back with all the love she still hadn't spoken out loud. Time to remedy that.

She broke the kiss and whispered in his ear, "I love you so much. You have no idea how happy I am right now."

He didn't have a chance to respond because right then the front door opened and every one of the Hartleys filed into the already crowded store. Each one of them wore a big smile. The men slapped Ben on the back in congratulations, and the women pulled Mandy into a succession of excited hugs.

"I'm glad to see you didn't mess it up," Sloane said as she hugged her brother.

Mandy must have had a curious look on her face because Ben took her hand and said, "I've been practicing that for a week. These two," he said, motioning between his sisters, "wouldn't let me anywhere near here until they were satisfied I wasn't going to muck it up."

Mandy smiled. "I approve of their instruction."

Ben smiled back, causing her heart to flutter. Would his smile always do that to her? She couldn't wait to find out.

"Although he still hasn't managed to put the ring on her finger," Angel said.

Without a word, Ben lifted Mandy's left hand and slid the beautiful ring onto her finger. In what she hoped was a good sign, it fit perfectly.

"That we didn't help him with," Angel said. "He picked it out all on his own."

Mandy looked down at the ring then back up into Ben's eyes. "I love it."

Ben pulled her close. "Mind if I kiss you in front of all these people again?"

"Not at all."

And he did, quite thoroughly.

"I hope we have a dozen kids, a bunch of little girls who look just like their mom," he said.

She smiled, marveling at how quickly a life could change. "I wouldn't mind having a few little cowboys who take after their dad."

Devon suddenly called out, "Fifty percent off yarn for anyone willing to make the happy couple baby clothes or blankets. Sounds as if they're going to need them."

Mandy and Ben laughed along with everyone else. She knew in her heart this was just the beginning of many laughter-filled years to come.

And to think it all started with a wayward pigeon. She'd never loved a bird so much in her life.

Chapter Fifteen

Mandy sang along with the pop song playing in the shop while she worked on a new display in the front window. She felt sort of like one of those impossibly perky cartoon heroines who spontaneously break out into song while going about normal everyday tasks.

But there was good reason for that. She was happy, happier than she could have ever imagined possible. Her latest checkup revealed the baby was doing well, thankfully her morning sickness had been short-lived, and the shop was having its best fall season ever. Of course, that could be partly due to the fact that it seemed every knitter in a fifty-mile radius was making blankets and baby clothes for her as if she was having septuplets instead of one baby. She'd already received so many knitted and crocheted gifts that she'd announced she'd be organizing donations of extra items to charities that helped mothers with babies.

Arden had helped her research various charities and pick a couple. When they'd visited a shelter in Austin and met some of the women and children there, Mandy was hit anew with just how lucky she was in her life.

Sure, her dad had abandoned her and her mom, but he had never physically hurt them. And they'd never had to live on the street or run for their lives or wonder where their next meal was coming from. She knew then and there that even after she had her baby, she was going to keep the knitting program going and draft seamstresses, as well, to make items that could be used year-round. After all, the season when knitted items were comfortable to wear was shorter in Texas than most states.

And then there was Ben. Her heart filled to bursting when she even thought of him. In the two weeks since he'd proposed, she'd watched him gradually become more comfortable with being a father. She could not wait to see their baby in his arms. Each day her love for him grew, and she had been accused of walking around with a perpetual smile on her face. She could live with that.

She sprinkled the silk fall leaves on the floor of the display window, around the baskets of yarn skeins in both fall and Christmas colors. Well, that looked cozy and inviting, if she did say so herself.

She turned to reorganize the chairs she'd moved out of her way while she worked, but the sound of the front door opening drew her attention. Expecting a customer, she was surprised to see Arden instead.

"Hey, what brings you by? Writing an article on the scintillating world of knitting?"

Arden smiled at that. "While tempting, I actually wondered if you had a few minutes to talk."

Curious, Mandy motioned toward the seating area

frequented by the knitting ladies. "Sure. I could use a break anyway."

Once they were seated, Arden scooted to the edge of her chair. "I would like to run an idea by you, but I want you to feel completely free to say no. I will totally understand."

"Okay."

"What would you think of us having a double wedding? Neil said you and Ben are wanting to get married soon."

"Yes, before I'm the size of a houseboat."

Arden smiled at that. "Neil told me he'd wait however long I needed, but I'm ready now. I don't want you to feel like I'm stealing your day, though. I just thought—"

Mandy reached over and gripped Arden's hand, halting her explanation. "I think that's a great idea."

Even though she'd been the one to voice it, Arden looked surprised. "You do?"

Mandy nodded. "I'm so happy for you and Neil. He worships the ground you walk on."

"I feel the same way about him."

"I know."

"You and Ben are the same."

Mandy smiled. "We are. That's why this is so perfect. We've all been through so much. Celebrating our big days together—well, it just feels right."

"I'm so glad. I think Diane and Andrew will like it, too. But what about Neil and Ben?"

Mandy thought about it for a moment. "You know, despite the fact those two tease each other unmercifully, they love each other, maybe even more than brothers who share blood. They'll never say it, but I think they'll like the symbolism of it. Another bond tying all these unrelated people together into a family."

"Now you sound like the writer." Arden reached over and wrapped Mandy in a hug. "I'm so glad we're going to be sisters. I always wanted sisters when I was growing up, and now I feel like I hit the sister lottery with you, Sloane and Angel."

Mandy's crazy hormones got the better of her and tears pooled in her eyes. "Me, too."

"Oh, I didn't mean to make you cry."

Mandy waved away Arden's concern. "Puppy food commercials make me cry now. It's like my hormones have developed a personality of their own, one that wants to keep tissue companies in business."

Arden laughed at that, and then they were both laughing as they began planning the biggest day of their lives.

"DUDE, BREATHE," ADAM said as he leaned toward Ben at the front of the church. "If you don't, you're going to pass out before Mandy even walks down the aisle."

On Ben's other side, Neil, dressed in a similar black tux, chuckled. Ben glanced over at his older brother.

"How are you so calm?"

"Oh, I'm nervous, but I'm more happy."

"I'm happy." He was, really. He just felt like he might throw up, too.

Neil looked at him. "You love Mandy, and she loves you. Don't think about anything else."

Great advice. Now if he could just put it into practice.

After years of thinking he'd go through life alone, of convincing himself he was okay with that, he was on the verge of being a married man. But instead of being nervous about that, he was more afraid that Mandy would suddenly change her mind and not show up at all.

As the music changed, signaling it was time for Arden and Mandy to make their appearance in the church's sanctuary, Ben took a deep breath. Adam, who was serving as his best man while their dad served as Neil's, clasped Ben on the shoulder and squeezed.

"Almost there, bro," Adam said.

The doors at the back of the church opened and there stood Arden dressed in white on the arm of her father, who couldn't possibly look prouder. Beside Ben, Neil inhaled a quick breath at the sight of the woman he loved. Happiness welled up inside Ben. Neil and Arden deserved this.

It felt like it took forever for Arden to reach Neil, for her father to lean over and kiss her on the cheek before taking his seat beside Arden's mom on the front pew.

The music changed slightly, and Ben was almost too scared to shift his gaze to the back of the church. But he slowly did and his breath caught. Mandy stood there looking like an angel, his angel. When she smiled, he felt it all the way to the deepest part of himself, to the frightened little boy he'd once been but was no more. He was a strong man who was going to do everything in his power to make the woman walking toward him on her mother's arm happy. To keep her safe, to keep their child safe.

Everyone else in the church might as well have disappeared because he had eyes for no one but Mandy. His heart beat faster and faster the closer she came to him. When she finally arrived, her mother touched his arm, drawing his attention.

"Take care of my girl."

"I will."

Then Mandy's mom shifted her gaze to her daughter. "And you take care of him."

Mandy's gaze settled on him. "I will."

When Mandy took his hand, he felt a tremor that probably matched his own.

"Nervous?" he whispered to her.

"Yep. And I have to pee."

He couldn't help it—he laughed out loud. It reminded him of the night of the movie in the park, the night of their first kiss, when he and Mandy had laughed so much that those sitting around them had shushed them like they were rowdy kids in a library.

The laughter helped him relax as the ceremony progressed. Neil and Arden said their "I dos" and sealed their union with a kiss. Then it was Ben and Mandy's turn. He somehow managed to repeat the vows, slide the ring on her finger without dropping it and keep their kiss PG-rated. Okay, maybe PG-13.

"Stop trying to outdo me," Neil said, and everyone in the church laughed.

He knew wedding receptions went along with weddings, that the brides and their mothers loved them, but all Ben wanted to do through the entire thing was scoop his new wife off her feet and take her to bed.

"Let them have this," Neil said as he sank into a chair beside Ben. "We've got the rest of our lives with them."

But as he chatted with family members and friends, he couldn't help wishing the rest of their lives would start just a little bit quicker.

When it was finally time for the happy couples to make their departures, Ben couldn't keep his hands off Mandy anymore. He pulled her close and kissed her as though they were outlawing kisses at midnight.

"Get a room!"

Of course it was Greg who'd said that, making everyone laugh again. Ben looked back at Mandy, who was blushing.

"Watch this." Still holding her hand, he searched the crowd for the perfect way to get back at Greg. He smiled when he spotted her. "Hey, Verona. I think you need to set your matchmaking talents to work on Greg."

"What a good idea," Verona said. "I need a good challenge."

More laughter floated through the crowd assembled to see them off. Except from Greg, of course.

"I almost feel sorry for Greg," Mandy said.

But then they stepped outside and saw Ben's truck. In addition to the expected string of cans trailing behind it, the entire thing had been wrapped in pink streamers. Complete with a huge pink bow affixed to the front grille.

"I take it back," Mandy said.

Ben just laughed. Nothing was going to ruin this day—not his past, not the doubts that had long plagued him, and certainly not having to drive through Blue

Falls with his truck looking like he'd crashed it into a cotton-candy factory.

He motioned toward the truck. "Shall we go on our honeymoon, Mrs. Hartley?"

She smiled and lifted to her toes to plant a sweet kiss on his lips. "I thought you'd never ask."

Epilogue

Mandy heard someone's quiet voice murmuring as she woke up from what felt like the deepest sleep she'd ever experienced. Man, she was tired. She felt like she could sleep another week and still not be totally rested. She supposed that was what twenty hours of labor did to you.

As she blinked away sleep, the voice took on a familiar deep rumble, though he was obviously trying not to disturb her. She slowly rolled onto her back so she could see Ben. When she saw him holding their daughter close and looking down at her with pure love and devotion, tears welled in her eyes. Until this moment, she'd evidently still harbored some level of worry that Ben's doubts about being a father remained.

Watching him gently boop Cassie's tiny nose and say "Who's Daddy's perfect little girl?" put those fears to rest for good.

She didn't know how long she watched them, but it was obvious that both man and baby were totally in love with each other. Cassie waved her little hand in the air as if trying to touch Ben's face, so he leaned down and let her. Cassie made one of those happy baby sounds, halfway between a coo and laugh, that was guaranteed to make people smile and forget all the bad in the world.

Ben finally glanced toward Mandy and smiled. "Look, Cassie, Mommy's awake." He stood, holding Cassie close like he would protect her from entire armies single-handedly. And Mandy had thought she couldn't love him more. How wrong she'd been.

He carefully placed Cassie in her arms then brushed his hand back over Mandy's forehead, smoothing her hair away from her face.

"How are you feeling?" he asked.

"Tired but happier than I've ever been."

"I'm so sorry you had to go through that."

She shook her head against the pillow then looked down into her daughter's blue eyes, so like her father's. "It was totally worth it for this little beauty."

Ben pulled the chair up next to the bed and clasped one of Mandy's hands. "Thank you."

"For what?"

"Making me the happiest man alive. For showing me that marriage and fatherhood are not things to be feared." He brought her hand up to his lips and kissed her fingers. "I love you so much, Mandy. You and Cassie."

Her heart expanded with joy. "I love you, too."

More than any words in the universe could ever express.

* * * * *

If you loved this novel, don't miss the next book in Trish Milburn's BLUE FALLS, TEXAS *series, coming September 2017 from Harlequin Western Romance!*

Of all the towns in Texas Poppy White could have chosen, she settled on Stonewall Crossing—the town where Toben Boone, rodeo cowboy and father to her son, lives...

Read on for a sneak preview of A SON FOR THE COWBOY, part of **THE BOONES OF TEXAS** *miniseries by Sasha Summers.*

Toben carried the large white box with breakfast treats back around the corner. He knocked on the shop door, smiling at the boy who opened it.

"Can I help you?" the boy asked, all brash confidence, boots and a shiny belt buckle.

"Got a breakfast delivery from Pop's Bakery. Welcome to the neighborhood." He held the box out.

"Thanks, mister. That's real nice."

"You a cowboy?" an older, sullen boy asked.

"I'd like to think so," Toben answered.

"If you're a cowboy, where's your horse?" the girl asked, hands on her hips. "Don't real cowboys ride horses?"

"Sometimes they drive a truck, like your aunt. She's a real cowgirl."

"She's the best," the smaller boy said, smiling at Poppy. "Four-time national champion. Third-fastest barrel racing time ever. Onetime international champion—"

"Oh my gosh, Rowdy, do we have to hear it again?" the girl asked. "We get it. She's awesome."

The younger boy glared at the other two. "You don't get it. Or you'd think it's awesome, too."

Poppy placed her hand on the younger boy's shoulder. "Thanks for bringing food. I'm hoping once they're fed, they'll be a little more civilized."

"I can't wait for them to go home." Rowdy sighed after the other two had left the room.

"You get to stay longer?" Toben asked.

"Nah, we live here now."

Wait, was Poppy a mom?

"Better hurry before they eat it all," Poppy said.

The boy ran from the room, and Poppy sighed. "Listen, Toben, he hasn't figured out who you are. I mean, he knows your name—but…" She shook her head. "Just let me tell him you are…you. Okay?"

Toben stared at her. "You lost me."

"Rowdy knows Toben Boone is his father. But you didn't introduce yourself so he doesn't know you are Toben Boone."

Toben felt numb all over. "Rowdy?"

"That was Rowdy," she repeated.

"I don't know what you're talking about, Poppy. But if you're trying to tell me I'm a…father…" He sucked in a deep breath, his chest hurting so much he pressed a hand over his heart. "Don't you think you waited a little long to tell me I have a son?"